Love & Thanks
for all your support
Denis.

Maximus and the Golden Web

The Lion of Persia
Book One

written and illustrated

by

Denis Rosair-Antoine Bouchard

edited by

Renata Simkus

Maximus and the Golden Web

The Lion of Persia

Book One

Canadian Cataloguing in Publication Data

Bouchard, Denis Rosair-Antoine, 1953

ISBN: 978-1-928030-00-3

The Writers Guild of America
Registration no: 1577507

For Maximus

Denis Rosair-Antoine Bouchard

Born in the small town of South Porcupine, Ontario, Denis grew up in a world of dreams replete with depth and textures inherent to a simpler life. The northern landscape suffused experience with a profound connection to the spirit of nature; informing the complexities of his work as an artist. From inside the silence of meditation he has journeyed the expansive mysteries of meaning; the infinite qualities of humanity in all its colours, dramas and nuances. The story of Maximus and the Golden Web came to him on such a mystery; the witness of how a small dog, an Italian Greyhound with a crooked smile, brought joy through his innocence to all who met him; their troubles forgotten in timeless encounter. After one such moment on a cobbled street in Mexico, Denis returned to his studio where among the easels and brilliant pigments he began to paint with words as Max settled himself onto a shawl covered chair and watched.

Maximus and the Golden Web

1837: Dreams inspired by village myths of ancient reservoirs, waters buried by centuries of shifting Bedouin sands, draw a Persian boy into the desert to stumble upon a stone lid. He and his grandfather discover the carved granite conceals entry to a mystically charged world entombed for thousands of years. Once opened the crypt breathes softly, spiraling life into its depths awaking artifacts from ancient Babylon laid to rest in dead silence in attendance for the first of true souls to come. Brought into the light of its new world the tomb releases its power to four winds.

1921: The young Bedouin, apex in a lineage responsible with protecting the ancient Babylonian trust, devotes his life shepherding the contents of the crypt into the world following the aegis ordained by ancient reason; the treasures rejoined into a small shop in Venice, Italy. For near one hundred years, the antiquities are kept safeguarded in unwitting trust, locked in mystery by the proprietors and vanishing walls of "The Crystal Rose".

Spring 1928: A mystical talisman is entrusted to a Duchess by an exogenous visionary embodying masterful prophesies lit by a daytime moon. One month later, four invitees leave a grand castle in England for an old family friend's home in Barcelona; the Duchess, her sister the Dowager, their guardians embarking on a journey unrivaled. As they step onto the train bearing them to Paris through a veil of steam, in Venice an unsuspecting American traveler is transformed by the rain into unwitting guardian for a sarcophagus, one of the portent antiquities holding within its intricately carved gilt box a key to awaken treasure; new life beginning its final journey to auspicious reunion with all others of like inspiration.

In Paris France, the Hotel George V gathers in two groups of invitees called to the Villa *Jardin* to await the arrival of the last of their party. Time rests in preparation for the last leg of the journey to Barcelona on which the appearance of an ancient magus in a dawn lit train corridor sparks intrigue; another awakening.

In the gardens of the historical villa the Duchess responds to the spirit in a small dog; opening herself to visions of ancient Babylon and the magus walking together with the tiny creature delicately prancing on four legs. Trapped by this foresight her soul is bound to the little hound. Caught in a weave of fantastical threads she travels away from the villa to her home with other invitees; all without *souvenirs* of encounters in the magical gardens that had welcomed them save the Duchess her profound grief at losing connection with the little one her host had explained away as inconsequential; deemed flawed by awkward smile and rounded dome crowning amber eyes.

One late night at Bennington Castle a knock opens to an elaborate gift box teetering on the castle stoop; its belly trembling with the unexpected; toppling the little imperfect dog Maximus to spring into the arms of his Lady. Centered in the joy of the embrace the visionary's talisman regains its incarnate soul igniting the power worn about the dog's neck, jeweled collar of exquisite beauty inlaid with precious cabalistic symbols reuniting with the life of the spiral echoing secrets engraved on the Babylonian granite seal; rebirth of the future unfolding the New Golden Age into the care of the Chessman.

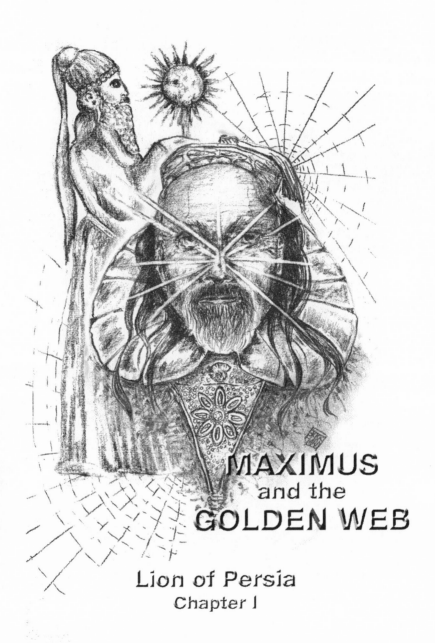

MAXIMUS
and the
GOLDEN WEB

Lion of Persia
Chapter I

the Chessman
... red velvet night crown of electrodes
drawing out the last of his dreams.

Chapter One
The Lion of Persia

The Castle on the Hill

Depleted from an unsettled night, the Chessman rolled from side to side, legs tangled, pinned by the weight of silken blankets and nets of hounds' legs spilling across his bed's end; red velvet night crown of electrodes drawing out the last of his dreams. Removing the bonnet, his morning voice whispered commands to the monitor waiting patiently on his night stand. *"Display the harvest sleep has gathered from unconscious."* To the canopy above his head, the dream exhibit area opened; musical accompaniments tumbling from the bedposts. He lay in silence as images from sleep state flickered about in pinwheels of visuals like those of old silent films, encapsulating what his subconscious had imprisoned these many years.

In one scene he could but discern in a line of gently blowing laundered sheets brushing the likeness of his mother, a much younger woman than he remembered, plucking lettuce from the garden she tended so carefully under the kind eye of the man she shared her heart with.

Present amidst a rapidly growing stream of pictures, captive in a parade of stills, were flipping pages of photo albums

3

painstakingly depicting how his youth had prepared him for this life of solitude; sentinel in service to changes larger than one life. He watched still amazed at how the device could access so accurately, extracting from his brain's cells what had been for so long forgotten, haphazardly sold off for other memories, seemingly more pleasant, more present.

Throughout single windows, easterly panes caught Jack's intrinsically beautiful breathy plumes. Such crystalline feathers were unusual for this time of year, worrisome. The morning sun rising slowly to the back of leafless oaks that lined the hill to the property's end glistened through where Jack's lips had incidentally touched glass faces. The Chessman smiled, finding that bits of joy reflected from within the waves of frost ridged in the transparencies liquefied as the sun ascended; its beams of warming light curling around the crowning majestic. He missed Jack; etchings exhaled in so careful an archetypal script.

Resting his head to his pillow, he watched as myriads of swirling images dotted the canopy as would night stars; reviewing treasures eclipsing one another as the computer released, folded over, each message orbiting, transmitted from its data base. He marveled at technologies, amazed at how the tiniest of terminals could draw from the human mind wave upon wave of memorabilia filed away in the deepest recesses of the sleeping mind.

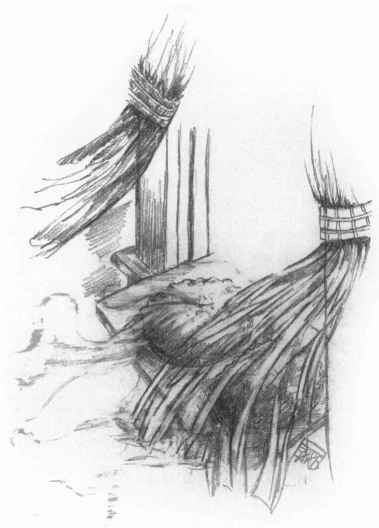

The kitchen sheers billowed,
dancing in a summer's breeze;
gentle sweets carrying the sugared scent
of fresh rhubarb and strawberry filled crusts ...

Each morning he woke to this external land of dreams reminded of his past. Those he had so loved as a child, sleeping suspended within the silken threads of this machine, carried him off to a small town at the base of the hill where human existence made up of a simpler life enabled souls to journey beyond the hill's top. Hoarded thoughts of other lands, times and space seen from a veranda rocking chair grew within imaginative thoughts lifted upon the distinctive perfume of cooling pies.

The kitchen sheers billowed, dancing in a summer's breeze; gentle sweets carrying the sugared scent of fresh rhubarb and strawberry filled crusts through an orange doorjamb that glowed a defiantly strange loneliness. Beyond its threshold, he felt the invisible threat of cool nights as his grandmother walked the halls, her nightgown brushing the floor, tossing light caught from the full moon into the wide eyes of a child bundled against the dark. Lost were these daughters to these centuries' old ideals.

Down a short hallway pressed tight between plaster walls a bedroom door sat in its wont, ajar, swinging in tempo with the gentle snores of an afternoon nap. The boy tiptoed quietly to peek behind each cherished moment; encountering one room to the other, looking in on each memory as he had not for such a long time.

On a patch quilt, arms tucked beneath her apron, lay sleeping a crown of tufted grey hair; faceless image hidden beneath

On a patch quilt,
arms tucked beneath her apron
lay sleeping a crown of tufted grey hair;
faceless image hidden beneath faded ruffles of floral cotton ...

faded ruffles of floral cotton gently lifting to settle with every whistling sound of the one he had felt so dear. Quietly entering the bedroom to lift a soft corner of her apron, he peeked, wagering play. A chalk white face unsheathed, as still as death itself, remained unmoved by the sudden intrusion of day's light. Eyes crinkled to amusement, her knowing smile sent the boy on his way.

Today would be like no other, the castle walls would deify this force in a hush immovable to the unexpected; ominous cold sinking to those who slept deep beneath the gardens' ground. It would be a day satiated with unraveling secrets, most treasured for thousands of years, cradled within the castle foundations.

Delicate art no longer feathered the glass panes; etchings pooled to casement ledges. Jack with his crystalline kisses had melted away into memory, apace with the Chessman's dreams. Released from the attachments to revelation from this, his last journey with the dream catcher, expectant ear primed to welcomed steps as wet shoes echoed his caretaker's cope with the pathway from cottage to castle stoop.......

Released into the snap of cold morning's air, each click of a heel on stone reverberated with the metal clips whose sole purpose had been to preserve his shoes on long walks to school but in whose loud taps was the flight of professional dancers hoofing their way down old worn roads. The beat of quick steps brushing through garden stalks signaled a morning that had burst into mysticism enflaming the spirit of his initiate, coiling to run; watched in hallowed silence by those who had gathered.

Keys rattled the front door lock; sharp metal clicks traveling loudly through to the castle walls, drawing the Whippets from beneath their blankets to rush the halls in a tangled weave of bodies flying for the win. Outcries into loud howls of reception resounded in waves as the roaring crowd clamored over one another in competition for first attention. Past the castle threshold, they would run making their way to the garden leaving a silence spilling up the stairs to the Chessman's chambers. Fast in the bed, Maximus and his master kept the cold at bay nestled up; ritual committed to warm sacrament.

... primed to welcomed steps as wet shoes
echoed the caretaker's cope with the pathway
from cottage
to castle stoop.

... unfolded wings fluttering,
tips caught in the reflection of the sun's flame.

Persia 1837; a hilly desert covering the ghosts of Babylon ....

The heat was beginning to bury Layth; his clothes sticking to his spine with the paralyzing weight of dense perspiration. Crossing over the hilltop, looking for a place to rest he pierced the sands around him with the tall stick he carried, in hope to define a space, rest awhile in the shade of a stand of old palms that crowned the dune. He fought with the headdress he wore, sweat turning into heaviness laden with worry causing it to slide over his tired eyelids. Pressing back the loosened cloth, he looked up to the shadowed old palms, their broken plumes hanging to swing in what breeze would cross this desolation. A few more steps, sandaled feet sliding into shifting sands, brought Layth to a patch of dried reeds and grasses, the perfect bed to catch extending despair; his body slipping down into its comfort unable to carry the exhaustion that had left him unfeeling.

Relieved at dropping into a so longed for renewal he watched curiously as a butterfly, having been wakened from its stillness, escaped the hidden dark of his bed; unfolded wings fluttering, tips caught in the reflection of the sun's flame.

At dawn's break that morning Layth had heard faint whispers tipping his ear from inside a deep sleep. He woke to voices persistent in ancient conviction, disembodied presence unshakeable in the quiet dark that drew from him allegiance to purpose he would follow without reason.

It was said selected souls would cross through from parallel worlds, touch lineage dreamers with magic, connecting with their spirits to take them with before sinking back into the shadows of their time, purpose surrendered. Around gathering fires tales were told of those that had been lost to such visitors offering treasure. Truth lingered at the heart of these stories filling village boys with longings for great quests and Layth was no different, feeling pulled to a world found only in the persuasions of myth.

Mornings, he had walked for hours the land of his forefathers in tireless spirals, probing the grounds around him with the tall stick. He did as the whisperers had encouraged, their voices ringing inside his head, summoning him to listen carefully for echoes deep within the desert sands. Their promises of new life, the waters to be found, gave incitement to what would bring him every dawn to the hills surrounding his village. The tellers of stories had warned that voices from beneath sands could be false with intent, not giving up treasures easily; leaving unfortunate believers lost to the village but to Layth who unknowingly carried family links forged in centuries lost to time, they had passed on visions of ley tunnels, webs running through dreams rich with fresh waters.

Layth had followed those dreams into the drought; seeking life, finding all had been mercilessly thieved leaving behind wasteland and endless oceans of sand. He sat exhausted in the shade of broken palms; their brittle crooked fingers locked in anguish for this land no longer blessed. In the cruel demand of sun's anger, the weakened shade of this place of rest drew others to join Layth in its subtlety; tiresome chatter of ancients' voices pooled in limpid song, turning over in nymph-like vocals.

Incomplete silence unlike any other, precious quiet vibrating, flowed over this bone-washed place of hilly Persian desert accompanying dancing grains of sand whirling about; bits of buried cities. A voice distinct to night's time whispers called Layth from his day of purpose into the opaqueness from which the butterfly had risen; the place extending meaning beyond life. His grandfather had once told him these wings of delicate tissue served to bear the love of those no longer exerting force of life; reaching through the barrier of confinement to those living from whom they had been torn.

The voices from his dreams held Layth's hand as he drifted off; pillow of reeds beneath him a chariot into phantom worlds. *"Beneath your feet those most ancient sleep; once great civilizations, the powerful, embracing greed, creating wars, came to fall from grace with their gods; vanishing from sight. Gods on earth, they built a towering city, erecting temples of breathtaking beauty, encrusted in precious stones stripped from earth's veins, every inch more spellbinding than the powers of Egypt."*

This desert wonder grew to such majestic heights, rooftops spilled over with gardens so lush that uninterrupted streams of visitors walked lured by the exquisiteness that had been forged from dusts of unfertile desert lands. Elaborately dressed, jewels glistening in the bright day's light, their gilded horse drawn carriages rolling the stone roads, foreign travelers perched atop deliberately concealed cargos; behind flowing silken veils, wealth of unimaginable proportions. Afoot through the dense traffic, the enslaved, buried in dust incense, concubines, handmaidens and menservants followed in procession beneath large brightly colored parasols.

Threading this magnificent magical tapestry of intensely vivid color were visitors of lesser wealth from as far away as the Phoenician colonies. Above all heads, in the distance, could be seen taller expansions of white carved marble, pillaring supports of lofty extensions pushing the surrounding city walls back to rise even higher; reflected into great sculpted pools of still waters emerging from inside palace gardens. Mirrored in liquid calmness were those inhabiting these tiered dwellings; drenched in clouds these towers housing Emperors, their queens and priests, all communing with heavenly Gods.

Visible throughout the city standing alone up to the barricading walls tall buttressed platforms loomed, their steeples adorned with magnificent blue-breasted birds, skilled trainers astride their backs readied to journey, sighting the Great Wonder from the bird's eye view. The travelers between extended wings, holding reins of gold laden livery, set sail, headdresses of crystal and slivered cooling amber guarding them against the blinding sun-rays of day; the molten silver of moon, stars and night planets. Like kites guided through mists of hanging clouds these rare gentle creatures tipped the cities' impregnable beauty; soaring over terraced gardens gripped in the hands of omnipotence. Undisturbed by the astonished inspiration of spellbound onlookers engaged by such unexpected magic, the riders guided the birds to circle the Tigris and Euphrates river banks; following groves of date palms whose ripened fruit flashed like jewels to grace their shores. *"Wonders beyond understanding such as these have been lost to unforgiving deserts, reclaimed from those without value for life; woe brought upon they who demanded fair measure for others but did not give such measure themselves."*

Sleep's cessation under the stand's thin shadows ferried Layth to memory; tales of wealth and beauties held in trust by village story tellers. He had dreamt of these lost cities, their hidden chambers presumably filled to overflow with great treasures of gold and priceless artifacts; corridors of polished marbles mirroring reflected images of palace inhabitants passing stealthily, their rich garments swaying gracefully across the coolness of stone floors. Carried off by fantasies, throughout extraordinary opulence, down masterfully carved hallways, he walked over thresholds into rooms of shelves staggering under the weight of objects so plentiful; tellers of stories would themselves tire of the recounting.

... travelers between extended wings,
holding reins of gold laden livery, set sail;
headdresses of crystal and slivered cooling amber
guarding them against the blinding sun-rays

Inset gems,
the palest blue of tears,
flashed the texture
in his soul;
hair of flame
spilled over shoulders
shrouded in profound sorrow

Once as a small child centered alone in the fading threads of an adventure being spun, Layth saw himself walking, dusty feet and naked ambitions carrying him to the bottom of a staircase; eyes following curving stairwells of illusion to the edge of darkness, where they met the alabaster form of a lone man.

Inset gems, the palest blue of tears, flashed the texture in his soul; hair of flame spilled over shoulders shrouded in profound sorrow, arms crossed, cradling infinite patience. From within these simple folds carved of fine linen, long pale hands delicately reached down to a table manifest, its polished surface scattered by fragments of curling parchment. Without looking up, the tall thin man of stone beckoned Layth to approach but in the way of dreams Layth fell away into waves of scented wild flowers; rippling blossoms kissing the feet of palms that had fallen like defeated soldiers.

Dried plumes above his head whispered him awake onto his bed of reeds; arched back stretched, bringing him to fully sense the rebirth of ancient time. Pressing tight his lids to open, he sat up crying out a heartfelt plea to these dwellers of sacred grounds, "*Lift this curse that has imprisoned our land these many years.*"

This blinding ball of fire light spilling across desert sky had once given life but grew to curse the land as it had everything beneath his limbs. Turned to ash were those he had met in the shimmering smoke of gathering fire tales, grown to love; realities lost in refusal to reform, devastation returning in waves of debris.

Layth smiled to himself at the insanity projecting inside his eyes, lids red, feeling to squint into the mid-day sun. Lifting from this expansive tomb of sand was a heat so intense it could bend the air he breathed; sifting shapes of mist from distant shores. He felt to his hip for the goat skin pouch he had kept closely guarded for years; his common tie to supernatural powers.

This was gifted him long ago by a passing stranger of fair complexion who in pressing the cool disk to his hand advised him to secret. *"If you believe wholeheartedly as I, within this round of crystalline resin, you will find magical powers."* In the presence of this stranger, Layth had seen the alabaster man; the creature who had offered him view of curled parchment.

Reaching into the small goatskin bag, pulling on scraps of tightly wrapped linen, Layth readied himself to free what he had shown but one other person. Having evidenced the gift to his grandfather, he told of the man who had passed through the village that day saying, *"This lens of polished amber, once peered through, will uncloak the lies the deserts carry within intensive heats. Its magic is in that it sees as you will, cutting through the haze of solar rays to truth."*

Once having witnessed the magic in the stone the Elder believed what the stranger had told his grandson; taking comfort in the wisdom nurturing within Layth who in respect for the stone would keep the treasure safe from prying eyes. The boy would take care to move beyond random sight before drawing the stone from its hidden place to press it onto his own brow unlocking the mysteries of optical illusion.

Resting over his eyes the gift's power opened itself fully allowing Layth to travel beyond illusory truths as they rose distorted from walls of mirage. He saw mystical visions trapped by the desert's heat; the amber freeing them from its embrace. He remembered well the coolness of resin to brow when nights came to join day and he lay in his cot, arms and legs spread out like a star, darkness resting with the weight of the stone on his forehead; an emperor's crown, one bigger than life. In the still of the room through this amber shield he could gaze directly into the soft glow of the moon surrounded by her empowering jewel-lit skies, freed from lingering fears and doubts. His gift had many times magically carried him off to be touched by those from the Silence; carrying him off to join in dream with lands as barren as these settling beneath him, ancient beating hearts drumming rhythmically with his own.

Into the needle-like shadows that cut across his resting limbs loomed thoughts of a strange nearby haunted hollow years ago abandoned by the village; caught to the recesses of Layth's mind. Recurring memories of his father digging through a tall cupboard's back pursued him many nights into the ante-room of sleep, as they had since the age of four. Once his home, a bed of ash and sand now bitterly marked the burnt out site with the skeleton of a tall blue weathered open cupboard, awkwardly leaning, still filled with old pots and pans. He visited the site often, never entering, clearly remembering.

Hidden in the unwieldy bones of old shelves was a loose wooden board; door into unimaginable darkness through which Layth had grown as damaged as the remains of a home at the edge of a road, awkward as the structure that stood as he had, alone, outwardly uncaring. The fire that had destroyed his life, taken away those he loved, had managed to calcify the vulnerability of boyhood.

Unable to share frightening images of that night, his parents abducted, a horrific sadness had settled to his breast over years; silent tears strangling his heart. Grim shades of men of same face, driven by rage, terrorized his innocent mother who self-sacrificed to intruders aggressively holding her husband. This had carved into his soul, severing loving ties, destroying life as he knew it.

Through a hail of shouting, past screams fighting for life, Layth crawled under a nearby table towards the blue cupboard's bottom shelf where the tunnel his father had dug waited to orphan him. He had done just as his parents had told him.

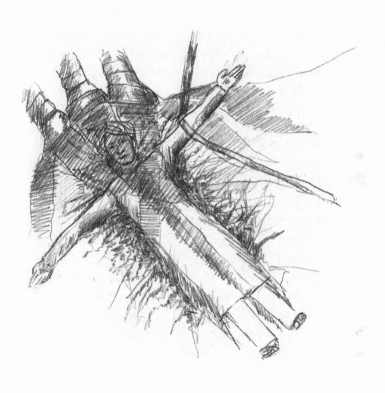

... arms and legs spread out like a star

*... the skeleton of a tall blue weathered open cupboard,
awkwardly leaning, still filled with old pots and pans*

"Within the hollow you will hide, disappear magically, staying safe until our return. Behind this cupboard lies a world unlike any other; this loose swinging plank our answer to your safe keeping."

He remembered the numbness filling his limbs when his mother bade him hide; those from his dreams coming to life in his mother's voice. Once inside the safety promised, though near petrified of what could spill over from angers boiling, Layth turned to face the brutality waging war against the spirit he so desperately clung to.

Peering through a narrow slit in the board that gently swung shut, terrified as shouts escalated, vision blurred through a wall of tears, he listened to the ransacking of the house; abuse of his parents continuing.

Two of the intruders furiously pulled everything from walls, strangely passing over the cupboard; staining him with the guilt of survival as their destruction consumed all else. What Layth feared most came to pass, his mother and father bound, wheeling from distress, were forced to camels' backs; one last scream of horror disappearing to the night sky.

The one man with glistening rings, picked up an oil lamp, hurling its flame across the room; criminal rage bursting into heated roars as fire tipped to the dry woods and cloths that lay strewn about floors. Layth pushed back against the earth cut by his father's digging, filling with want and need, forced to pull away from the heat, curled to watch the cupboard's back as flames slipped through its crevices like snakes' tongues. Life vanished before him with the intrusive assault, his parents never to be seen alive again.

Here on this hillside, Layth lay in the quiet of the afternoon held in remembrance to an old blue cupboard standing alone as he had all these years, backed by a darkness his father had so carefully hidden behind it. His mother's delicate touch, soft scented hands caressing his face, reassured, *"In future will come a night changing our worlds forever. Keep worry at bay, for it paralyzes thought. Unable to speak of this night to others you must trust that in future you will know all has been ordained by ancient reason. Heart of hearts, more than jeweled sentences these words are, for we all, your father and I as well, will be here next to you, guides to what has been promised."*

It was that very night they slipped from his life; she the one who had shown him love so deep and now lost, gone forever.

He was but four when he watched curiously, his father spending days digging out a tunnel through the back wall; all that was left of home, reduced to ashes and ripples of fine grained sands. The charred remains called him back by day-dreams and night-tosses to stand as awkwardly as they did; deformed, filled with numbing memories captive as the old pots and pans teetering on slumbered shelves.

More than a decade had passed since that strange, terrible night which surfaced only at times like this when half asleep, dazed by shards of sun or moonlight cutting through palm fronds or bedroom shutters, would Layth slip off into recurring dream-like flights of vulnerability, held to worlds of tears and goodbyes.

Arching his back to a cool passing breeze, comforted by his bed and the reassurance of courage prevailing, he daydreamed to the precipice of sleep where he would feel his mother's comfort wrapped in a scent of delicate spices colored of saffron.

A loud thud resonating deep earth tore him from his world of dreams with force disconnecting. Rubbing away tears blurring his vision, Layth was brought to his feet looking for what had thundered across the hilltop; finding only silent palms twisting their scorched hands. The hilltop unchanged, he reached for his stick to find nothing save a depression in the sand where he had forced it deep beside his bed of reeds.

Looking around he saw the staff, teetering on the surface of something solid to the foot of another incline. In what magical world could this have happened; deep burial wrenched from earth to light such a distance away. He stood for a moment reclaiming the staff; senses trembling as he leaned down to touch what lay on the ground, half exposed to the day's light, projecting from a pile of stones and desiccated palm fronds. Scraping away what he could with the tip of the stick, he shook with excitement as from inside the crust of debris a curving edge glistened.

The earth beneath him began to move, lifting as if alive; sudden quake firing pinpoint streams of light, sparking brilliantly, debris flying, whirling about his ankles and legs, spiriting off in huge spirals. Burning with anticipation, Layth was stunned with filaments of pinching sands that spun in to buckle his legs. Magical air whooshing up around him swelled his clothes whipping his head scarf from him; dropping him to his knees.

The wind died, releasing its tight hold on Layth's eye lids; allowing him to risk the dangerous cut of sharp sand when he opened his eyes. What he saw was in the way of dreams, a gilt domed stone cap of ancient design, jewels exposed, covered in delicately carved inscriptions perfectly preserved.

Staring deep into the wonder, he held speechless as thoughts tumbled, untangling in his mind. Was this an answer to his pleas for survival of the village or a sacred place rising to engulf him? These sands embodied secrets that whispered loudly, calling Layth to task he could not yet see. Closing his eyes, seeking clarity of vision, forehead to the dome's face he breathed in ancient scents.

He knew the labyrinth in dreams wove threads of intrigue leading him to follow what must be. Struggling with heat threatening to bury him again he sat to his heels determined to gather the best out of exhaustion. What he could not know was what had awakened beneath the butterfly's wings.

What he saw was in the way of dreams,
a gilt domed stone cap of ancient design,
jewels exposed,
covered in delicately carved inscriptions
perfectly preserved.

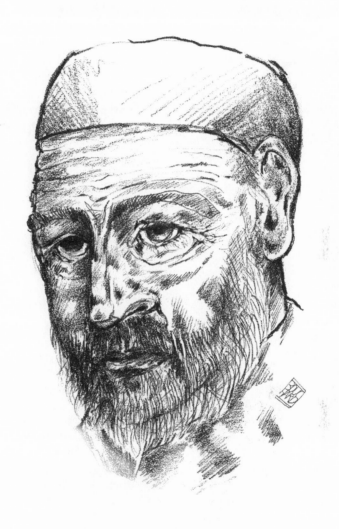

Laws of the Circle
Chapter II

Chapter Two
Laws of the Circle

The Castle on the Hill

Coal cinders burnt out in the fireplace at the foot of the bed. The stars and moon that framed the mantle through open drapes vanished with the breaking of the day's light. The Chessman had lived in his castle surrounded by ancient artifacts. He seldom slept. When he did, this player of life's mysteries would wake to the sound of delicate symphonies spilling from floating transmitters that danced about the bed's canopy. On the table next to him an illuminated screen leaned awkwardly over piles of books and note papers.

Technologies of this arc in time, for the better part, he had left behind. He preferred what he knew but did at times take advantage of these amenities. *"Bed, lift me thirty percent,"* he said, preparing for the adjustment. *"Mattress, rise to my right and stop when I say to. Blankets move to the foot of bed, stay covering my feet until my initiate comes to join me."* With that he lay waiting, bathed in the modern comforts of his bed sitting room hoping that this day his caretaker would be on time.

From his chambers he heard the dogs rushing the castle halls. As they neared the front entrance in a roar of barking and howling, he felt relief at the familiar jingling of old keys. This all made him remember the day when the child he had been was summoned by those from the Silence to great work.

Maximus his hound stayed curled at his side beneath his own velvet blanket. His hand resting on his companion he listened for the muffled footsteps that came every morning. The years of walking the pathways in the Spider Garden were coming to an end. *"Today perhaps,"* he whispered aloud, *"may be my last. My initiate grows in her strength and soon will she be able to see us through to the Golden Age. Upon return from our time with the Snake of Orpheus she should read for me again. I miss my friends, especially Layth."* He closed his eyes; *"such a lion ... to have led us all ...... "*

The rubble spilled in every direction,
rising up into ghostly shapes.

Persia 1837; the Layth story continues ....

Wild cries fired from inside a huge mushrooming cloud; its thick dust turned over folding into itself. The rubble spilled in every direction, rising up into ghostly shapes. Stones clattered over the narrow pathway as the enormous mass pushed on downhill.

"Allah Akbar ... Allah Akbar" beat from its center. Through the drumming of desperate feet it kept rolling faster and faster, the sphere swelling, discharging flashes of light shattering the darkness of its impenetrable wall. Released from its shell a boy burst out into a courtyard that had been lying quiet. Sand and dry earth clashed with the air transforming into waves of particles that shimmered; fused under the touch of the sun.

"Allah Akbar" echoed across the yard through the walls of a crumbling dwelling. An old man startled from his prayers lifted his head from his rug. Under the assault of enthusiastic shouting, to a nearby casement he moved. Struggling with a rusted latch, he pulled open the wooden shutters that blocked the day's oppressive heat. Blinding light entwined with choking dust slipped through the window, cutting the darkness that blanketed the room; sudden glare pinching the old man's lids. Cupping his eyes, he squinted through the haze; searching in direction of the boy's familiar cries. What had called him from inside his deep meditation was an unfamiliar timbre that rang clearly to the old man's spirit.

Layth stumbled forward, freed from the shroud of dust that trapped him; the cloud continuing to roll into the dense heat walled in by the courtyard. It thrust itself well beyond the boy transforming into huge gossamer wings that fell snaking around Layth's shoulders. They unfurled into magnificent glistening sails before bursting into the sky; shimmering filaments dispersing like crystal threads of delicately woven silks.

Layth coughed. Fighting for his voice, he coughed once more; his torso twisting, hand rising, shaking of excitement. He pointed towards the hilltop crowned by a stand of yellowed palm trees leaning defeated by years of blistering heat. Stammering, he gasped, *"Grandfather I have found it. You must come now."*

His grandfather, Elder of the village, had prophesied that waters needed to sustain life would soon come. Clouds did come yet left nothing save the desperate fears of drought. The villagers were deeply connected to the land beneath them. They could draw waters from any source, heaven or earth, but no blood could be drawn from this stone. Layth knew the old man struggled with self-doubt; fearing he could no longer read the promise of inspirations. In his search for water, Layth had hoped to find his grandfather's lost heart.

Layth's cries had cut into the Elder's silence. A note in the boy's voice had carried secrets from the hilltop; ancient song passing through into the Elder's meditation, lifting the burden of unfulfilled prophesies. Something inside the boy's voice had sung into the old man's spirit. He reached for his cloak; pulling as it caught on tiny slivers of wood bristling across the table top.

At the door he drew in his thoughts; disoriented in interruption from deep meditation of prayers great in importance. The sight of his grandson winged at the foot of the hill bridged the depth of prayer to the light of this day. He remembered other days the boy would run into the village spinning with extraordinary stories. Layth's tales were most often met by walls of disbelief. With the mantle of prayers still upon him, the Elder could now see their alignment to mythic ancients. Before stepping out into the glare of the courtyard he looked inward for guidance; closing his eyes.

Adjusting part of his head cloth over his mouth he looked up feeling a rush of dust laden air press by him through the open door. He knew he had closed it before prayers. Bemused, he continued to cross its threshold into the still air outside which hung silently around him, unwilling to move. Reaching back to pull the door closed, he jumped in shock as it slammed shut with a disturbing clatter without cause of sudden wind to move its weight.

Turning away to the other side of the courtyard, confused, he whispered to himself, *"What mystery has the boy carried down the hill?"* Strangeness consumed everything about them as it had but ten years ago.

Even though he held the cloth to his face, fine dust seeped through to cloak his lungs; filling his chest as had smoke from the flames that destroyed the boy's home. Layth had survived, having hidden himself behind a large blue cupboard. The boy never spoke of that night which had become an invisible part of village history. Because of fears that gripped the village, speculations of what had caused the fire were suppressed. It was simply agreed that ill fortune had struck the family and that chance had drawn the boy to safety. Such things would be spoken of at times of gathering but strangely none spoke of this fire and of how this boy had lived. All but the old man accepted the imposed silence.

Layth's grandfather driven by need to understand what had come to pass had stepped through the charred remains to come upon evidence of the tunnel dug by his own son. He guessed only that this had saved the life of his grandson but the old man could not fathom the purpose that had driven Layth's father to undertake such a work. Layth had survived but was never the same. The old man was left to grieve alone.

Other losses further threatened with endless droughts worrying harvests, violence creeping the river's banks to erupt into terrors feeding on greed. Foreigners had come in search of ancient treasures. Their insatiable appetite for those things ancient, wondrous of this world, spread like a plague to leave the land pocked from archaeological looting.

Barges with extreme wealth belonging to Persia and her dead floated unchallenged down the rivers and out to sea. These treasures journeyed for months to foreign lands; greed swelling beyond human hearts deep into the land itself. Rivers would rise mysteriously in furies, taking back what had been ripped from sacred grounds.

Foreigners who came to Persia in search of their own purpose served native greed as well. Those hiding under the cloak of protector had laid siege to villages along the Tigris River. Their claim of securing desert lands against aggressive pilfering of artifacts and heritage was widely acknowledged among the desert peoples but whispered of as something other. The truth was these magicians who said they fought off foreign thieves, they themselves assisted in the rape of treasures from the sands. Mistrust choked the region; fear escalating. Attacks on innocent villagers stopped everyone from daring to confront the evil. From this the Elder protected the boy. He would always come when Layth called and so he hurried across the courtyard. *"What has happened? What is wrong?"*

Layth ran towards his grandfather, took hold his hand and jumped up and down pointing towards the path. *"I have found it. We've no time to waste. Come, we must go and now! I have found what we have prayed for."*

*Layth had survived having hidden himself
behind a large blue cupboard.*

Unseen forces pulled the Elder into the boy's frenzy and the two started to run up the narrow path. His heart raced as they climbed one incline to another. Beside him Layth's emotions spun wildly off into the day's heat. The boy's chatter wound them both up tighter. He spouted off about miracles, the greatness of Allah and what they had been given this day. Everything became wrapped in frenzy; Layth's excitement whirling about them squeezing at the old man's chest. The boy charged with boundless energy pulling them both with relentless force up the hill until Layth came to stop. A flood of silence deafened the hilltop.

The old stand of dry palm trees stood alone surrounded by grasses and debris. In the stillness Layth struggled to speak. Smiling broadly he pointed towards his staff lying on the ground, partially buried in a pile of colorless straw. The Elder studied the hilltop questioning the strange nervousness it held. In the wild run up the path he had lost all sense of what had pulled him from his prayers to this barren spot.

Layth leaped past him, dropping to his knees at a mass of sticks, branches and straw gathered along the crest of an incline. He pushed frantically at the pile of material then clawed the blanket of debris, throwing wildly in all directions. His grandfather, held back by his years, watched as Layth brushed away the last bits of cover to reveal a stone disk.

The energy that had gripped Layth began to slip away; drawing him back on his heels to leave him staring blankly at what he had discovered earlier that morning. The suffocating heat of the day had continued to take its toll. They both remained in heavy silence until a rumbling traveled the ground, forcing Layth to his feet.

Scatterings of sun bleached grasses began to snake atop the sound that grew from the earth beneath them.

The loud thunderous noise pushed up through their bodies. What grew into guttural sounds of anger moved the earth into violent shudders. Grasses trembled and shook, rising above them in a giant twisting of debris. Old palm leaves mixed with sand lifted by unknowable forces curled, curving into a great shelled dome, its rounded roof cutting the light of day. Darkness fell as night. The old man threw himself to protect the boy; Layth reaching for him, they held one another tightly. Their headdresses took flight joining the mass that whirled about their limbs.

Time stopped in the fury of the storm. Debris rained down to rise again above them forming a massive wall blocking out the clear blue sky. Afraid to risk the storm's returning rage, they stayed curled on the ground, arms locked around one another. The storm slowed in a hail of screams turning on the wall, dispersing it.

The energy that had gripped Layth
began to slip away

The whistling fell off and away as Layth stood to help his grandfather steady himself. In silence they questioned what had consumed the hilltop. Emerging from what had concealed them, they were spellbound by the golden dome which revealed itself fully in the most intricately carved inscriptions. Exhausted, numbed by what had come from the storm, Layth's grandfather stood, arms lifeless hanging from their weakened sockets. He remained simply staring at the stone. No matter its beauty, he was incapable of feeling.

Layth's eyes rose to see a strangeness cross his grandfather's face. Though the Elder had felt the assaults from tides of mystery, his faith protected him with disbelief. The boy had accepted these same tides to know with certainty that he had been led by ancient design to this sacred stone. While he could feel the depth of his grandfather's fatigue the whispers of the morning had woken Layth to destiny. Of this he would convince his grandfather.

"Grandfather, would you believe that we would have you taken from your prayers, run faster than your years to see a simple stone?" He straightened, reached out and touched the old man's shoulder. *"Have we not been praying for water? Over the years clouds have come and drifted away without leaving behind a drop of rain. Have I not searched every day the hills surrounding our village following the call of prophesy? Could this not be what story tellers have spoken of? Grandfather, I was led here today by those who guide from inside dreams. The ancients have called us. Here this day it might be we change*

life's destiny."

Layth's eyes gleamed with reasoning as they met his grandfather's. The old man smiled, leaned down, held the child's face, *"Well named you are for you do so roar like a lion."* Straightening the damp clothing that twisted around his tired body, the Elder placed his arms reassuringly about his grandson's shoulders. *"Perhaps, after all, an abundance of waters could run here where we stand. Sealed deep beneath these sands, out of the sun's reach, they may not have dried up. You are right. Let us not feel defeated. May be you have found the entrance to buried ley tunnels such as have been spoken of. We may yet walk as they did thousands of years ago the corridors that flow with waters but we must have proof."* As Elder, he understood the feelings in the village to be brittle as tinder. Layth searched his eyes but within the caution he saw the renewed confidence his passionate argument had lit.

He placed his arms around his grandfather's waist; holding him near he felt his strength return. Silence around them fell away, leaving them to their task; the old man turning to survey the incline, kneeling to examine the seal. He reached out to touch the stone. As he traced the inscriptions on its outermost surface his fingertips dipped past the gilt. A liquid light rose then fell to the shock like shards of a full moon breaking across a still pool. He shuddered as the blood of the stone took hold of his hand traveling his veins to flood his soul with mystical communion.

An eruption of divine knowledge blinded him to the desert hilltop leaving him staring dry eyed into timelessness of prophesies. Sacred provenance was here entombed under this dome within fantastical pictorials serving the Laws of the Circle; Effect born of Cause, carrying both destruction and peace. These perfectly preserved encryptions shone; overpowering the mid-day sun and the sensibilities of the old man. What had shown itself this day was not of this earth; must be of dreams, only of such.

Layth searched his grandfather's face for understanding. The stone was blinding and it was clear the old man could no longer see as before. The boy reached inside his cloak for the pouch he always carried. He retrieved his cherished sliver of amber stone; carefully unwrapping it. Taking his grandfather's shaking hand, Layth pressed the disk into his palm as once the stranger had done for him repeating the words, *"If you believe as I do, this gift will hold magical powers."*

He guided the old man to place the translucent disk to unseeing eyes. Layth stood by to watch as his grandfather's soul took leave. It was as he had been told about those passing from the earth. The sun worn face no longer embodied feelings or emotions. An ethereal peace veiled the familiar beloved face which took the light of amber reflecting the glow of the stone itself. Sight returned and the old man spoke.

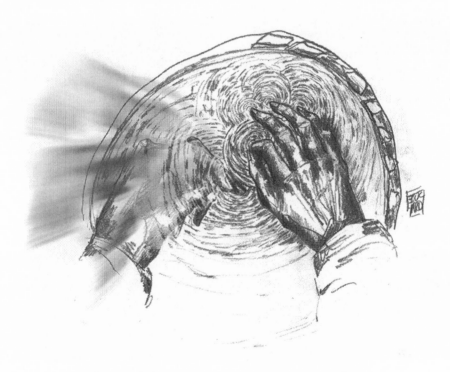

*As he traced the inscriptions on its outermost surface,
his fingertips dipped past the gilt.*

"Thank you my son. This is truly a magical gift for now I see with a different clarity. What was founded in truth has opened its proof to me here mirrored in this polished form." The Elder was spellbound. Reflections within the glassy surface penetrated to lands of dreams and worlds existing but unseen. Encrypted here were endless codes and symbols that human eyes alone could never see. The amber, gift from a stranger's hand, revealed itself as no mere stone but truly a tool of power. It illuminated the meanings carved so long ago by those who set the dome to seal what lay below.

Evidenced in the inscriptions were all wonders of the world, kingdoms of the sun, queens of the moons, royal beyond countenance. The Elder suddenly felt himself carried off in a great jeweled chariot of knowledge. He felt himself completely blind but could see, understand all. Unwelcome tears gathered on his bottom lids streaming down his cheeks. He feared missing anything.

Through a haze of activity, a magnificent black stallion appeared in the traces before him rearing, its mane like a long beautiful sail rippling across the deep blue skies. Seduced by this extraordinary essence of beauty, the Elder wheeled his horse drawn carriage through the vision, unaware of the realities that surrounded him. Off into other worlds, he traveled deserts to dreams. He had never seen so vividly this land that slept between imaginary lines; such fantastical images, breathless and unworldly, this nautilus filled with all that had existed since time began.

Layth's impatience cut through the vision; echoing across the hilltop. *"Could this be water?"* Without turning, the Elder extended his arm, placing his fingertips to the boy's lips, carefully studying what was scripted at his reach. What had been carved in these passages on the inclined dome told more than an ancient story. Then wonderfully, sand encircling the dome began to ripple; every grain glittering as did stars in the heavens, dancing away to reveal yet more of what was to come.

More than the earth had moved since he was pulled from his prayers that morning. Layth's call had changed his world; Life's relevance becoming clearer. An incorporeal spirit had taken him over to the depth of his soul. Blinded, the Elder no longer saw as he desperately tried to grasp at more fleeting visions spilling from unseen presences. What the silence carried in its dazzling embrace was a power neither evil nor dark. Without form the substance that touched his trembling hands foreshadowed signs he wanted to remain with, believe to be true. In the stillness of soundlessness unearthed, he would listen endlessly to ancient whispering voices caught in the folds of the desert's breath.

a magnificent black stallion appeared
in the traces before him rearing

Rising from the Tigris
Chapter III

Chapter Three
Rising from the Tigris

The Castle on the Hill

The Chessman listened to the chant of his initiate's keys as she climbed the narrow stone path up to the castle stoop. He had watched her day open; unfolding into hours unseen by nature, ordained by time. From the silence of Ancients, through his own, traveled the guardians. This gift and many others would open the gates of heaven, fulfilling his promise that she too would walk the pathways as had he.

He had lived in lands beyond memory, traveled backs of birds unseen by human eyes for centuries, conversed with a god of waters, the one the Greeks called Oannes. This deity, like the Chessman, thought to teach that which was divine to humanity. Like those before him, the Chessman would share with Imled what was needed to protect oneself from the Eye of Evil. What envy would destroy with a malevolent gaze could be outdone by love above all and only with such.

From that time in Mexico, brought to look after an old man come to read the histories carved in the stones of her homeland, she had taken on the sacred task of keeping safe this teacher. Leaving the wells of her people in service to this mission, unknowingly guided by his care, she became his apprentice, next in succession to carry burdens and the knowledge of precious wonders. This cold morning he had closed his eyes to watch her transmigratory soul move through manifestations that guided her mastery. This morning he had closed his eyes and watched her become what she was to be. He smiled, knowing all she wanted was to be on time for him; the Chessman who lived on the castle hill.

Held in the gardens shadowed by ancient invocations, through a maze of numinous visions, enraptured, the initiate felt the true statement of her strength. Imled accepted that the Chessman had chosen her for some secret reason. What bound them was love of all things most beautiful seen and unseen. Though flowerless, leafless, these grounds surrounding her were no different. Continuing her walk up to the castle, she lifted her arms in glorification of flakes of snow that began to fall from the skies. Plucked by invisible forces, purity dropped from the heavens to her lashes. She peered through the frozen lace that sparkled as would stars fallen from the blackness of a cold winter's punishment. Her shawl's fringes danced, touched by the gentle tugging fingers of sleeping plants bordering the stone walkways. All she had ever wanted to do was to take care of the old master.

Feeling this a privilege, she loved him as she would have loved a grandfather. While she tended his needs, he often spoke to her in riddled sentences, cryptic as the world he lived in. His bejeweled presence presaged the revelation of mantic secrets. Under this cloak of eminence and majesty beat a wildly compassionate heart, shaped by wisdom. He had taken the measure of her lineage but trust, in his way of thought, was something to be earned and with the years of attendance she had done just so.

Over long years of research and study the Chessman had accumulated the lore of all wonders, been into the heart of Silence and learned the language of the Earth and those who are other than human. Entrusted to his initiate, this would set aflame her sibylline lineage giving her the unchallenged strength the new age would need. She had learned what was desired of the many parallel worlds traveled by the secreted societies; coming to understand the interplay of form and thought.

Nearing the door, Imled lost the sound of the hall clock's chiming. It had for years rung the quarter hour but now its piercing echo fell dead against the castle inner walls. The strange bitter cold that tightly gripped her began to let go. What soddened the lower window panes, the sun's rays, cut through the trees that crested the south hill of the castle gardens. Still heavy shadows crossed the stoop as though protecting some of Jack's intimate works. His crystalline hieroglyphs, like tears, began melting away in light of the defiance of Sol. The retelling of keys announced her arrival at the door, sparking the descent of the household hounds.

As she fiddled with the lock, the caretaker felt eyes upon her. Looking up to see if the Chessman was at watch, she saw only the faintest of candlelight come from the sills of his bedchamber windows but she felt herself pulled to her left to see a tall mysterious figure rise from the shadows. Crossing the terrace towards her, a pre-biblical vision, its long flowing robes whirling about, floated, cradling something in white oversized hands. What it held in palm was the visage of the castle's own small hound formed of crystal. Gleaming from its transparent interior were ever changing reflections. A frisson seized Imled as she faced an antediluvian smile; its liquid moving through her as if to take ownership of her soul. Left in its passing was affirmation that she held full knowledge of ancient wisdom and the continuum of events traversing future, present and past.

The figure carried the crystal hound, she all else. Her spirit marked these secrets as true; cabalistic, cryptic symbols such as those carved into mountains of ancient Maya stone. She slipped the key into the lock releasing the dissonance of loud wails and barks, the excitement of paws from the other side outweighing her efforts to open the door. Moments fell away; letting her feel the joy, knowing their excitement would bow to ineluctable circumstances. The roar folded over into a skittish silence, the caretaker's touch of the handle triggering anew the cacophony of delirium.

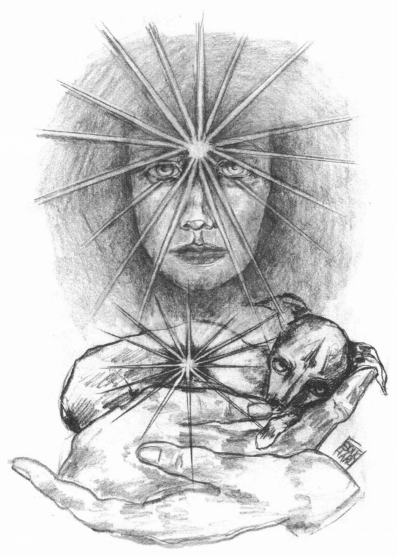

... held in palm
was the visage of the castle's own small hound
formed of crystal.

Laughing Imled pushed again at the door which gave way to the rush of yelping whippet bodies that piled up over one another through the narrowness into the day's light. They ran as quickly as they could past the initiate, hurrying into the garden. Propelled by their barks and growls, in one great effort, the stream of tumbling bodies rolled to avoid those few that stopped to jump and shoulder her. The caretaker continued to laugh as she would, trying best to survive their onslaught of ends over ends. Ten to the pack, breaching to overthrow their own energy the dogs up righted, displaying remarkable acrobatic feats.

Every morning and night when let or fed, the torrent would surround her; skirling, snapping, re-emerging to go off as they had come on. No boundaries to the garden paths, they would run chasing squirrel then scatter they would about the castle grounds parachuting its four corners with boundless energy. She waited patiently as usual, held to the door's stoop. Unusual was the air they ran about invigorated. Heads, tails, poked up through the countless carved lines of boxwood. Bodies alike, curiously bent around, stopped suddenly as if something would be seen emerging from the endless maze of garden walkways. She thought perhaps it was this incorporeal being, the ancient soul that had passed through her, which the sensitive hounds could see still hovering the grounds.

One by one, Imled greeted them on their return, counting heads as they passed to enter the castle. Making their way over the stoop they looked back cautiously to ensure themselves that the others were coming, no one would be left to the cold but under a communal nervousness they still readied to turn and run at a moment's notice.

First to line was Scout with his anxious expression, next Mabelle, fearlessness backed by her admiring Finnegan, then rushed, came the others pressed by the cold, Emma, Madonna, Toto, Hugo, Matisse, Hazel and as always late, full figured Manon, freed from the blows of the weather, head down, tail tucked, filled with worry that she may have stayed too long at play. Imled closed the door gently behind them and herself while the hounds ran the stairs tripping over one another in a race for the warmth of their beds.

In his quarters the old Chessman rose from his bed. Pulling his bed-coat from a small chair near his night table, he draped it over his slender fragile frame. He made his way across his room to the glass bathing closet. Slipping off his dressing gown, then night clothes, he entered the misting case that had been pre-programmed for full cleanse. Closing his eyes the Chessman watched his initiate as she slowly climbed the well of stairs to the hall's end following the hounds that on this morning had burrowed, gathering under the blankets to the foot of his bed.

Once the infernal machine dried and moistened his body he stepped out and spoke gently to the computer manifesting his clothes. Standing to the mark X on the floor, arms lifted above his head, his voice-chosen frock descended from the ceiling to be deposited over him. A short walk through his hats, shoes and jewels, accessories were done. As she accomplished the last of her trek down the hall he would have powdered his face and kohl lined his eyes. When the door to his chamber room sang louder with musical notes spilling from the ceiling he turned prepared for his walk down to the kitchen and his may be final meal of fried tomatoes and eggs ....

Bodies alike,
curiously bent around,
stopped suddenly as if something would be seen ...

Persia 1837; the Layth story continues ....

When Layth pulled him from his prayers that morning, the old man knew the world had altered. A wild eruption of images manifested, sending visions pouring through fissures in dimensions beyond sound and sight. He grasped at the reflections streaming from the Silence which carried power in its embrace; power empirical in its presence, neither evil nor grace foreshadowed. Wanting to remain in the stillness of the stone where soundlessness held eternity he listened for the ethereal whispers caught in folds of the desert's gentle breathing.

Layth read the lines of his grandfather's face as they shifted through confusions of enlightenment. Awakened before morning, called to the destiny of his lineage from within dreams he had been guided to this sacred stone. Bound to the supernal, the elder closed his eyes and turned to the sky. Alchemies entwined with this person most treasured, the boy felt swept into the waves of knowledge his grandfather crested.

With one quick movement the Elder pressed his ear to the air seemingly reaching out to rising and falling notes. *"Do you not hear? Fine grains of sand collide with other elements forming ancient words of divine perfection. They tell me springs of sacred truth have dried up over years, turning fertile earth to sand. The forces that wish to define the face of Truth remain in heated violent dissension; storming the spirit of this planet. The words I hear are the pearls of truth. Relentless they are, for the ordered actions of man have chained the Great Wheel, pinning its axle, disabling Life's natural laws. Sources most damaging have conspired to shape our destiny; driving humankind into systematic destruction. If we do not free the Wheel the fire's lightning storm comes to consume us all."*

Layth had never heard his grandfather express thoughts such as these. The darkness he touched upon disturbed the boy filling him and the entirety of the hilltop's space with a paralyzing intensity. What was concealed within the warnings frightened Layth, triggering glimpses of that night and the vanishing of his parents. Recurring flashes of what had been witnessed from behind the cupboard that night of fire brought on breathless fear. The same terror that had gripped the darkness of the small house held him firm again in its clutch; his mind tightening around its nightmarish visions. Layth fought the drowning waves that would sweep him away on peaks of emotion; to bury him again, well to the back of the hollow his father had dug. Before he succumbed to the weight of darkness, the old man's voice pulled him away into other gentler prophesies.

"Leave your entombment," he said as though having been within Layth's thoughts. *"Fear not, for what foulness has been woven, Divine truth will undo. Mankind borders extinction. This has held since the beginning of time; little changing. Those that come from within Silence will intervene. They will tie the ends of extremity together causing cataclysm; collapsing days of unawareness.*

Worry not, humankind will be forced to regain consciousness putting a glorious end to mindless droughts, making soul lands fertile, rich, bright with a new golden age of evolution. Humankind will finally free this earth from poisonous greed which the love of human hearts will heal. What societies have raped of this world's wonders, from such ignorance a sign will emerge; the tempter of mankind will weep. A mighty blow will be brought those buying sin with sin for only what has been held in place by Divine order will endure; happiness will attain when regard for all creatures is held in like manner as all humanity might wish for self."

With brighter potentials thus spoken, the old man looked to the palms; surveying the bleak hilltop. He turned to his grandson with new thoughts. *"Angels, precious attendants to God, inhabit this place. Paradisiacal grounds here could once again surpass all other regions to become the ultimate authority of learning. What lands have been taken by oceans of sand may too be reclaimed for us by fresh waters."*

"This discovery of yours may be water after all but let us embrace caution. Our village has had much disappointment; perhaps cannot bear more. If this is an ancient water source lost for centuries it would give life to this land as it once did." He turned back to the stone, took hold of its edge. *"We must lift this stone; break its seal."*

The elder's hands shook, moving back and forth. *"Sites excavated by foreigners in the recent past have shown that this land was once so fecund that its inhabitants saw themselves blessed by their Gods."*

... he felt himself buried again,
well to the back of the hollow his father had dug.

"The myths of those times tell of how these people imagined themselves to be deities controlling life through birthright. Having the ultimate choice of openness or dark they chose the latter; hoping to sustain their appetite for that which could not belong to any of humankind. There are those who claim ordained knowledge of the unexplainable who accept these stories to be truth as mortals might have been blessed with extraordinary powers."

Stories such as these told at gatherings fired Layth's thoughts, filling his dreams with myth and majesty so rich in detail. The hypnotic sound of his grandfather's voice created realities of night that rivaled those of day. Where might the Elder have traveled to gather such information that could take the boy slipping off into a labyrinth of complexities?

"There are those who have supported and do support the existence of parallel worlds allowing music, wisdom, writing, magic and alchemy to cross all universes. Portals have always existed; doors allowing travelers to move from within Silence to this earth. I have known in my life some who passed through these doors being chosen; enabled to dip into what has been ordained by ancient reason. They have spoken of ultimate and divine energy manifesting to touch humankind without judgment, teaching earth's inhabitants to love one another. Perhaps such gateways yet exist, waiting for a time in which humanity will again open itself to accept each other, joining these teachers, these Keepers of Divinity."

The old man and boy stood together steadying one another as they looked to the stone. What the hilltop had revealed shone much brighter than before. Something more than what had seemed, its surface beamed rays of light from inside an ancient consonantal text. Hieroglyphs such as these the Elder's own grandfather had taught him to understand. He was amazed to see it here alive. This surely marked the dome as protecting something of great importance. Tracing the patterns in granite, he felt the rise in conflicts and unkindness that wakened here through profound tears locked beneath this hilltop. He could see why long ago gods would have forsaken this place but reflected in the stone was the might of what would overturn the inevitable.

"I feel the vengeance of gods. I see forsaken emperors seeking the wisdom of magi. There was one most often spoken of. Stories of his greatness exist even today. Trusted above all he kept the faith of all those who came to win and lose their power. He survived the fall of many kings becoming the last adviser to the powerful Emperor of Babylon. Bade by the emperor to demonstrate imperial strength and majesty he traveled as emissary to far lands using his magical skills and artistry to captivate curious minds. Through his journeys he gained renown as a teacher, Most Eminent Magus, showered with gifts of treasure and mysteries. Bestowed upon him by the Turkics as a measure of their esteem was his most cherished of all; a little dog as exquisite in feature as it was potent in spirit. Maximus was of the dogs brought from the land of Pharaohs. Bred in Egypt for centuries they were presented as a seal of Pharaonic approval. To be in possession of such a treasure was proof of kinship with nobility."

Most Eminent Magus,
showered with gifts of treasure and mysteries.

"With Maximus as his companion he descended on royal courts. The grandest of palaces filled to overflowing. They came to witness the Great Essitam whose appearance of translucent ghostly skin, hair of flame and piercing eyes of blue-green gave him striking command of the crowds. With Maximus cradled in the folds of his jewel-encrusted cape, he penetrated the crowds of onlookers. Cries of delight greeted the spectacle of the cape as it slowly swirled like liquid gold lifting Maximus into the air. Thunderous roars drowned the music of fanfare as the little dog sprang from his perch into the magician's waiting arms. Palace floors shook with frenzy as the cape rose even higher framing the intensity of the magician's countenance. People scurried in fear of their lives."

"This stone proclaims that great and wondrous beauty. I weep this new information gathered in the seeds sown by those long gone. These rulers of the universe who left the hells of measured time have sealed within Mother Earth the proclamation for those chosen of what will save the world. Rulers of these regions most likely created this; an entrance to a tunnel which could very well lead to reservoirs of water or chambers of wealth. Places of knowledge or life may be why these inscriptions at my finger's tip I recognize. Look there to the far right. Story tellers in my youth spoke often of such a likeness. That figure and those others are of the time of Assyria, mystical Babylon."

"Thousands of years ago prophets wrote foretelling of travelers to our earth. Extraterrestrials they were called. Unseen parallel worlds celebrated their birth, held them, keeping them safe until it was time for them to walk what was known to be the Hall of Gods. They touched those chosen gifting them with

immemorial memories. As the soul survivor of great Atlantis, this creature is said to have risen from the waters to walk these lands."

"From the Erythrarean Sea he would rise to teach mankind basic arts; agriculture, metallurgy, architecture, navigation, mathematics and natural medicines. Lord of the Waves, he is seen here his human torso wrapped in a fish cloak. Once having given the secrets of civilization to man he returned to his home; dwelling in oceans, the most fluid of elements; water. He swims here to us thousands of years later curled within these delicate cuts of stone. Here is his name Oannes. This fish-tailed god of two heads, one of fish, one of man, circled the first light of day. His image adorned seals, coins, scarabs and ancient reliefs of palace walls. Here he is himself as the Sumero-Babylonian god Ea said to have expelled himself from heaven to live amongst humankind. Dwelling in the Persian sea he rose daily from its waters until one day he was released from his mortal coil."

This story excited Layth because inscriptions of water gods he thought were a sign marking a holding place of treasure; waters precious to these deserts. It must be that one would uncover an oasis beneath such a seal.

His grandfather leaned forward to take hold of the stone with the full strength of his will but the circle of granite would not budge. No matter how hard he pried, it simply would not shift. Layth joined him but even concerted efforts failed. The stone was fixed; sealed by some unseen force standing them in defeat.

With one last effort of a mighty blow the elder dropped his fists to the lid's surface. Drenched in perspiration the Elder breathed in deeply; regaining his composure. Layth's eyes rolled over in tears. Thwarted by disappointment he could no longer withstand the oppressive heat. It held on with relentless weight, drowning his thoughts. The specter of the stone immovable hung around his neck like a great yoke.

Layth looked from the stone's surface to his grandfather's tired face. *"This cannot be some passage leading simply into darkness. This seal would surely protect something of importance; a shaft leading deep into the earth to a source of water. What could be more precious than water? Is water not as life itself, vital to all?"* The two resolved to meet the silence of the unyielding stone.

"Grandfather, this is held by more than weight of granite. Through what we have experienced I feel the truth of what you have spoken. That which this stone protects could be a resting place for something far more powerful than water itself. The ancients have kept this mystery safe from those who might prove unworthy. Mother said that one day I would understand what was ordained for me by those who guard the future. This is the day she spoke of. We have devoted ourselves to these events, shown those within the Silence that we are worthy. The Seal will open for us."

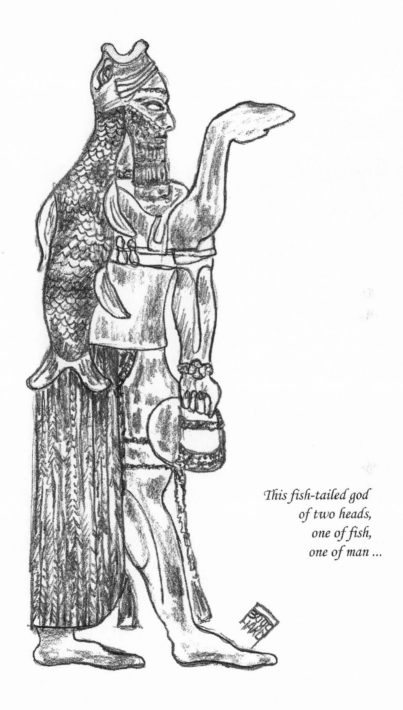

*This fish-tailed god
of two heads,
one of fish,
one of man ...*

LION OF PERSIA

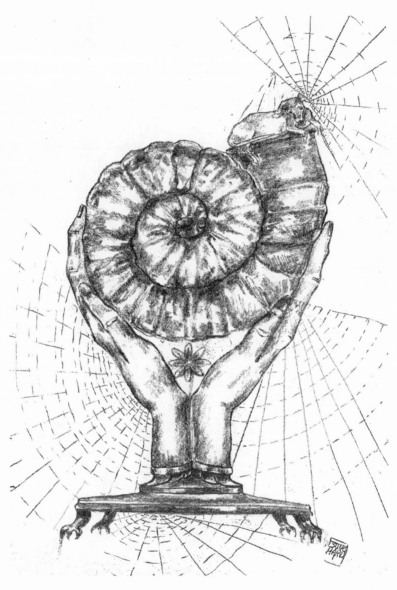

Phantom Tapestries
Chapter IV

Chapter Four
Phantom Tapestries

The Castle on the Hill

Imled stepped on the second floor landing to the quiet hum-drumming of a cleaning robot wandering about; bumping off table leg to table leg, intercepted by the wooden toes of door frames. She watched as it vacuumed past her. Changing direction the machine entered each room before re-emerging into the long hall that stretched out before them. The faint cloud of ashen dust that rose in its wake drifted to join years of fixed grey sediment coloring the wood paneled walls. Imled smiled to herself knowing the buildup left behind would stay undisturbed as was the way of the castle.

Dusty curtains of years pushed by the machine's exhaust wavered around her in dried molecules of the castle's genetics. For years she had walked these halls without seeing. Today the filaments gathered for her; tiny parchments of history tossed about like the ashes of those forgotten. Wakened from her dream, Imled was no longer blind to the messages encoded in castle fibers. Something yet unrevealed to the initiate had been trapped for centuries in this continuum leading down the long hall of past to present. Stretched before her in the gloom was revelation the castle had preserved for her future.

The past hung in endless rows of portraits punctuated by pillared arches into bites of history. Delicately carved frames, parsimonious with their luster, bore the weight of castle secrets, captive beneath coffered ceilings. Ghostly pale faces escaped the oils which held in stasis their likeness. Breaking through amber lacquers which could not hold back their life they watched Imled, their stares firmly denying her access. A beam of light broke free of the morning sun to kiss the lips and turn the corners of the Bedouin's mouth. His smile as of living crystal reflected bright destiny into the dark of each portrait's shadow.

Imled continued her walk under the lines of paintings through dusty beams of window light. Of silver, swords of polished blades, their edges frivoled away the gloom to the covers of curio cases sitting stolidly below the portraits. Old glass marred by frozen tears floating its reflections was encased in ribs of old wood, dust and webs. Artifacts beyond price were kept safe with hinges locked by the rusts of time. On this new morning she could see how each supported the spirits held in the frames above, those who had gifted them the castle.

Pouring from the Chessman's room at the end of the hall were brighter projections. Their penetrating lines crossed with those of the sun creating a tartan crystal wall that hung like stage curtains ready to unveil the next portion of her journey.

... a formless demand, tears swelling,
pressed time upon her soul.

Across the veil a formless demand, tears swelling, pressed time upon her soul. The loud squeak of her damp slippers pulled her back from the veil into the pantheon of portraits with the curio cases at their feet. Frost covered grounds had slipped into each step since she left the garden that morning at the castle's stoop. Gone unnoticed had been the faint growth of spirits' breath stirring deep from within the soils surfacing now to return her to the gallery of symbols.

Door after door slammed shut in ovation, a thunderous roar echoing off, filling the castle from foundation to spire waking the castle clocks. The walls which had fallen to a nighted silence reached out to what comfort the ethereal dust possessed. Bells struck out to the muffled beat of ten. Picking up her struggle Imled made her way back to the Chessman's door. Hammered sounds faded, falling to the shadows that clung at her back.

The castle cast off a new silence with dream-like whimpers of whippet hounds, doors creaking, reopening, one after another. The dogs buried beneath silken comforts remained untouched by the castle's altered field; their web of tangled legs wrapped in jewel toned cocoons of silk spilling from chairs and castle beds.

The Initiate felt all eyes upon her. Childlike expressions peered, straining to see beyond their gilded frames, looking for what would yet play out. Music continued to rain down from the coffered ceiling; silvered pearls spilling images to the carpet's pile.

Quietly turning her back to the Chessman's door she looked to each of the recessions for acknowledgment of all that had passed since dreams brought her to day's light. The faces in the alcoves leaning towards her in a panoply of cosmic consciousness, lifted their eyes from her to the bedchamber at the end of the hall; turning to the source of melodies reflecting dissonance.

The seal of life was evidenced in the questions unmasked by the creatures looking beyond her, freed from the poses set by the artist's brush. Imled followed their expressions back from where she had come. Mingled in amongst waves of musical sounds were emanations of Elysian whispers.

Accepting leadership of initiates, she saw herself to the Chessman's door. Looking through the crack in the opening she could see that nothing appeared to have changed in that protected space. With such expression overturning everything in its path what passed had stayed its course from the old man's chambers. The Initiate sensed something further unseen lurked in the faintest of shadows snaking about the Chessman's ceiling. At her back, the endless rows of concern returned to their familiar poses ....

*... she looked to each of the recessions
for acknowledgment of all that had passed ...*

Persia 1837; the Layth story continues ....

The pill of glistening perspiration broke free of Layth's brow; rolling down to sting the corner of his eye. The boy's lids held tight against the blaze of midday sun; holding in visions that had risen. Through the breaking dark of morning, voices of ancients called him to find this place of power where centuries had protected the stone seal that lay at their feet.

Beside him the old man tipped back on his heels breathing in slowly. Layth wiped opened his eyes to see his grandfather reach down with reverence to caress and retrace each of the figures carved into the stone's surface. He looked up at Layth, pausing in reflection, *"It would seem this find of yours could change our world. None must know what this day has brought until we have knowledge of its fullness. It would serve us well to take time; allowing our minds clarity of space to light upon the secrets opened for us."*

He laid his hand affectionately on Layth's arm. The boy braced himself as the old man pulled on his young strength to rise from beside the stone. They crossed the burning sands to where the bed of reeds, having cradled Layth in his morning dreams, beckoned them to rest. Worn by the storming images they had weathered, tired with efforts to shift the stone, they sank into silence.

The stand of old palm stalks, long dead, offered its

protection from the weight of the sun. Breezes were sent to sweep away heat, stretching shade across the two figures slumped in exhaustion; too tired to notice how the reeds held them in comfort.

They sat together quietly studying the stone lid that lay on the ridge facing them. Silence lay heavily, sealing them within the shadow of the palms' touch. Magic had cracked open the day revealing unfathomed mysteries but they could not know what was yet hidden within the afternoon heat. Having been pushed beyond their limits, they fought the crush that threatened their senses. An archer's breeze rose up, severed the grey clouds of fear that bound them. The feathered cool brushed at them, clearing the ashes of early day.

Spirit leavened, breaking his trance the Elder sat up grasping Layth's hand with decisive strength. Years fell away, he spoke with certainty.

"Reason in time is why we are here. What has traveled to us on desert winds is not of our experience but it is for this moment that our lives came to be. There is truth hidden in these soils. We will find life, a life of crystalline thoughts."

"There have been those who journey beyond worlds knowing this to be eternal, unchanged since time but the place of our lineage within destiny is to remain on this earth. Knowing only this world we stand vigil for days of answers to reveal celestial bodies, as many as these immeasurable grains. What rises, lifted

from where it has lain since the moon, stars and planets first appeared; blood of our blood. Beneath my feet I sense sacred elements have come to breathe effortlessly once more. Dimensions grow heartened. Consciousness finds its strength, girding anew in rebellion against those who might harm the life of this earth. I feel this fire rising through the heat of the desert into my limbs making ready for what we have yet to see."

"Mother Earth has loved equally both those living and dying. She cradles us now as she has cradled all existence, seen or unseen. Without condition, everything brims with her very spirit, all that is. I feel myself now filled with this intended force also. This planet, the Great Mother, has always reached out, calling for resolve and diligence to preserve that which has often times seemed doomed."

"Her expression has protected from violence this earth which gives us life. Within my eternal soul I see we have been brought here in accordance with the Laws of the Circle to act upon events; turning the evolutions of this world away from destruction. We will play a part in bringing these truths to the use of all who live. I know not yet what this part will be but it will be by our aegis to raise wisdom. Those who rule will understand the simple truth of natural laws."

Layth stared at his grandfather. He did not recognize this shape of speech. It was princely, weaving symbols into phantom tapestries. In this web he could grasp at threads of deeper meaning and so knew this to be the way of ancient oracles. This was not the way of his grandfather for the wisdom of a village elder was of ordinary times. His own consciousness filling with the spirit of the universe, he understood his grandfather spoke for ancient voices but questioned how well this manner of prophesy would travel amongst tribesmen. Years of drought and fear brought some to believe the old man's counsel without power of direction.

Layth tried to see his place in the enormity of what had been witnessed. His thoughts labored; falling into nothing. Eyes heavy under the weight of the afternoon heat, his spirit surrendered into a haze; slipping off his grandfather's voice into deep sleep.

Hand still grasping Layth's, the old man followed the boy into a world suspended, words scattered into silence easing him back onto the bed of reeds. Above them the date palms began to shiver in the cooling breeze; swaying to shake away death's long embrace, their stalks releasing years of desert heats as they danced with newness of life.

The Elder and his grandson sank into the comfort of this place, drifting beneath the sands into a dream of ancient thoughts wrapped in delicate images. Gentle breezes caressed the hill top with a seduction of temple incense. Like the whistling of wind through swaying palms, nimble fingers plucked the strings of palace lyres as man and boy floated down streams of tranquil peace suffused with exultation.

Sacred voices sang, connecting a breathless path through wonders of histories to a world bound in opulence. Iridescent wings trailing capes of bright colors proclaimed the gift of royal birds carried through mountains and mystery from courts of Imperial India. Tended by pious guards in saffron robes, sheltered in palanquins of jewel-studded yak skin, enigmatic beauties wrapped in vivid colors, one iridescent silver-white, were gifted Great Babylon. Received they were by a magician known to fashion wonders before kings and courtiers; his majesty crowned in hair of crimson red. From folds of mystical chorus, one voice stepped to front, *"Keep to the right. The bright one brought from the Far East embodies the truth colored of moon's light."*

Neither had dreamt so vividly before; one desert world abandoned, they journeyed with souls touching to wake in another shadowed beneath limbered palm fronds. Captive to the vision they walked through vast halls lined in many doors. They moved to knock upon these doors but found only one to accept their inquiry. It bowed; swinging open to a piercing light.

Tripping the threshold of a great chamber, they lifted their gaze, breathing in a vastness of space veiled in iridescent grey shadow. Gilt silver walls stretched up to meet a clear night's sky suspended over hundreds of light filled luminous pillars.

Like the whistling of wind through swaying palms,
nimble fingers plucked the strings of palace lyres . . .

Mirrored in their brilliance were thousands of reflecting stars spilling tensions of white and black tile floors. The polished squares mirrored the radiant full moon which, plucked from its stillness, fell melting from the heavens. Wrapped in undulating phantom mists she rolled through molten haze to pause at their feet, flowing into the shape of a great bird, iridescent in silver-white feathers. As she rose again to circle the two, her piercing kohl eyes gazed into their very souls.

Giant wings like those of angels reached up, absorbing every glittering star, gathering each of them as precious gems to her breast. A glorious tail unfurled, its cosmic fan stretching far beyond into the fireless skies. The two understood this to be protector, Guardian of the Gates of Heaven.

The peacock bade them mount its back that they might cross through dimensions of spirited form. Between dark mountains they flew; their way illumined by galaxies beaconed from the great bird's eyes causing unearthly shadows to be cast, pouring over earth and seas.

The floor of tiles that once mirrored the star dappled skies from which they had risen no longer held stars and moon but spread below as vast oceans rippled black to white. From within their swelling darkness, mighty Oannes himself had once risen, keening a soothing melody of gods; offering gifts of knowledge.

They journeyed over endless waves held to eternity, this giant silver-white peacock beneath them, carrying but one single thought between them; the hope of secret waters, fresh. Clinging to the coast, flashing below them were histories of lush green; pearls of lustrous fruit-dappled palm treasures. Embodying the blinding beauty of the Moon herself, the bird glided through the deep skies of night, rising on celestial winds to carry her travelers back from their ocean of dreams to reawaken on the sands. Keeper of consciousness, the bird bade them wake; its lamenting cries echoing through the mountains; dreams journeyed. One tender offering of iridescent feather tips swept away the last crests of fantasy.

Buried under them, deep within the dune a coolness was born of shade dripping from palm fronds rich with new life. The Elder woke gradually still holding firm to the young strength vital in his grandson's hand.

"These dreams have been a sharing of wonders. The haunting beauty that once graced the great Assyrian Empire has been entrusted to us through this divine experience. Approaching is a time when priests of this ancient Persia will travel other dimensions; journey back to us. I feel what pulses through these grounds is treasure entombed by gods themselves, kept safe by nature. Today we have witnessed her reawaken."

Between dark mountains they flew;
their way illumined by galaxies beaconed from the great bird's eyes ...

"In this journey of ours lies evidence of Civilization sending learned ones to conquer; harvest the knowledge of distant lands filling treasuries of arts and alchemy. Chief among lands undiscovered by these quests was a valley cradled between the sudden mountains of Khazaria. Their treasures, lost to time, will all return us now. Oceans of reawakening will again crest, crash to our shores, obliterating the fires of ignorance."

"Over many lifetimes, eons of doubt, marks of memory have been taken from our grasp, save the stories told of great mystics in possession of supernatural powers. These initiates, having protected this region from danger over millennia, ended their days of grandeur when emperors took this prowess to be of their own divine right and emanation; coming to curse these magi, expelling from their lands of being, burying them in disbelief. Suffering at the hands of harsh judgments, the ancient sages fell from grace through time as did finally the many civilizations to which their gifts had once brought ascendance."

"This history I learned from the father of my grandfather who, having mastered the art of storytelling, made rich our days and nights with tales of lost cities. We watched in amazement as he spun for us intricate adventures; reconstructing wars and endless conquest, enslaving those of neighboring countries."

"He told of peoples cradled within the crown of two mountains. Hidden from such violence, they reached beyond themselves to knowledge held by gods. They reached beyond their valley to become one of the greatest civilized nations of that time. Having amassed knowledge of tolerance, accepting all cultures the Khazarians began trading throughout the region, sharing the brilliance of their

89

banking and parliamentary systems."

"By the gathering fires we learned of the return to prominence of the magi. Most impressive were the endless recountings of the one magus known as Essitam. Not of this land, he was of Khazaria, the great city hidden between mountains. When his birthplace began to suffer that which had plagued the west his parents had cause to flee with their small child but for yet greater reason."

"Among peoples of nomadic tribes were those who possessed a deep rooted sense of things beyond knowing, of meanings encrypted within mysticisms and cabalistic symbols. Such is known even unto this day by secret societies kept hidden well from the view and threats of non believers. Inherent was this wisdom in the child Essitam. His parents perceived this truth, directing him to brave the teachings. They guided him to become an initiate of Babylonian instruction, trusting Essitam's gifts would be gilded into astonishing magic and alchemy."

"These he would weave into realities and unmatched wizardry. The promise of his youth came to pass as did his rise to be the greatest of all magicians. Notoriety brought him wealth of inestimable power as those of importance drew to him from all corners of the world."

"One evening a mysterious illness of mind overcame him. He took without proclamation the simple cloak of servants. The importance of his station was no longer seen on his person. None knew why he had been so moved or why he no longer kept his companion Maximus at his side."

"There did come a later day he would once again appear in court carrying wealth about his shoulders. A greater mystery cloaked the city when shortly after Essitam disappeared; vanishing, never to be seen again in earthly body. Those who loved him throughout the kingdom and neighboring countries were driven into deep mourning. His memory slipped away from most who had grieved; legacy left to gather dust. It was those gathered around the fires over thousands of years who kept him alive; changing us all with tales of his long and colorful life. Treasured were powerful teachings which became the center around all gathering fires. In our village it is by our own family hearth that his true place in the long line of stories is spoken of. Our family carries his lineage, telling forever of that which holds; all humanity will indeed be touched by this immortal being."

"It was rumored he would return one day. My belief as taught by my own father holds that stories of Essitam are not myth but of shared adventures, prophesies and a promise. It has been ten years since I have spoken of this promise. I have feared to lose hope for the future in all that has come and gone. I had doubt of the Golden Age wherein a great silent web would appear, weaving humankind together from all known worlds."

"On this day, in this place, we have seen things that I would have claimed full of lies. Under these old dried palms we have experienced things unbelievable. It may be that more than mere thoughts of this eminent magus will rise."

Above their heads vibrant green tendrils reached beyond dried stalks into the brightness of the day's lapis skies;

91

crooning of the many years they had kept vigil over the buried Stone of Ea. Giant birds wailed, temple dancers swayed, accompanied by the strings of ancient lyres. Layth almost heard the songs but he gave full heed to his Grandfather's voice. Neither he nor the Elder had noticed the palms were no longer parched. His grandfather continued.

"The fathers of our forefathers told of another Magus also groomed to be an advisor to Emperors. Essitam was foremost; his predictions considered to be of divine light. He walked through the city without thought for his eminence; adulation and love surrounding him. This influence worn so lightly by Essitam was coveted by this one he had undertaken to teach."

"His apprentice could see power accrued to his master and wanted this for his own. Consumed with judgments of right doing and wrongdoing his obsession blinded him to the ways and means of court expectations. Fraught over the meaning of life he fought to change the populace; outspoken, arguing his beliefs, preaching of the origins of evil in the world. Through this blindness the zealot incurred the wrath of those who ruled the city; coming to be feared as the Dark Magus. In distinction, Essitam his teacher loved and felt part of the society that revered him for his gifts. Dedicated to the healing of both mind and soul Essitam cared little for what he felt did not concern him. Working closely only with the nobility, respected by those of wealth and power he experienced his contributions as fruitful; his work as good and true."

"It is said the Dark Magus lived in needless turmoil until the end of his days; finding pain in the death of those he spoke of as most innocent."

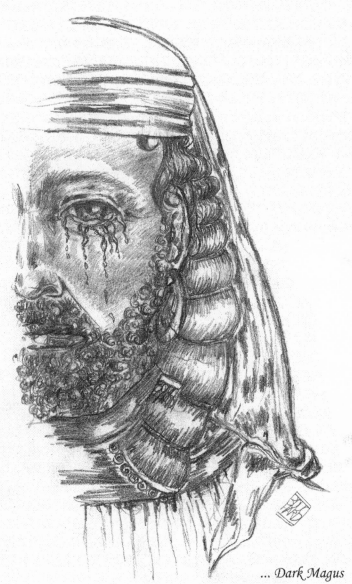

... Dark Magus
lived in needless turmoil until the end of his days;
finding pain in the death of those he spoke of as most innocent.

His struggle seemed futile for these masses feared to follow his teachings. He ended his days presumed banished. Tragedy spawned in the sorrow that both he as Dark, his teacher as Light, lived knowing each had the same end in mind. It was only their paths that seemed so different to those who could not know what is and what is not."

"Such stories of conflict remind us all may be lost into fires of hell when greed for money or power over others ignites. Allowing itself to be uncovered, this seal may offer to our world today that which is desperately needed; the salvation from the devastating cost of repeating history. Yet this day has been so full of twists, we may also find this place to be bottomless. The seal may be as empty of promise as many believe the stories to be."

"Let us go down into the village. The sun will soon be to advantage, reaching late afternoon. Once we have help from our village we can lift the stone; see clearly what was sealed long ago. If indeed a passage is found, we may have need of extra hands to undertake the work of entering. Voices in the air warn of danger approaching though I know not direction or source. It is best to have others here should there be risk in this undertaking."

Layth rose to help his grandfather cover up the stone seal. The two then made their way down the hill to what had previously been the center of their world.

Blinding Darkness
Chapter V

Chapter Five
Blinding Darkness

The Castle on the Hill

The Chessman could be heard shuffling about, his tenor voice lifting from operatic lines jumping to stern commands; musical memories, sounds of years past tumbling from bones of the house. All beings that had held their own court through time in this castle gathered in his chambers. They honored him for whom Destiny had written this day; from whom the Initiate would take her mantle. Beyond the spirit of milled oak timbers, within intricate runes carved in a familiar seal, bloomed the path from here to there. When flowers seed the time of life, greatest of prosperities, the student will carry the master home.

Having stepped across her cottage threshold that dawn, she left her past bequeathed to night. Dreams had reached through the moon; leading her into a much loved garden masked in unfamiliar alchemy protecting the grounds of the great house. Perfection most desirous, elements aligned, would bear her flame to right the whole; beginning, middle, end. This stately home, of once old rule, resonated with otherworldly elements rising to circle the light of day. A river swiftly moving from beneath the castle's foundation washed over her, releasing evidence of bitter cold; shaking castle windows with life marked by unrest. Ancient orders of unquiet rose in perfect rapture.

Supporting the continuous stream of overtures most glorious, this house could be heard breathing. Within subtleties of muffled breath within the creaks, this vessel's damning chill was cut. Those that had come of dreams, illusive kind, had sailed ethereal seas of myth and mercy to live here with the Chessman. His self imposed reclusive life was mirrored in the silence of the moon's face as she circled heavens surrounding him; intangible as the calm soul in his Italian hound's eyes. Maximus, of no ordinary breeding, of the line transmigrated to this place, supported human existence with color imperturbable. Dispossessed of fear, greed, ugliness, he ruled the Chessman's house as though carried by monarchs of ancient dynasty.

The castle hounds too had been bred here in legion bringing the hunt from woodland chase to castle plague, settling in to the quiet final chapters of the Chessman's life. Initiates, solitary travelers having few to trust, found sanctuary in those true hearts. In this the Holder of the Water Serpent would never be alone ....

Lost in a forest of souls tangled in bloodlines, a little boy stood to see beyond his pains in the glass shattered by invalidation. Tight fingers drawing in circles on the window, the boy saw his place in a world flooded with tears. Once cast upon the shores of unknowing, the burdens of his youth would be lifted. This he could not know.......

Tight fingers drawing in circles on the window,
the boy saw his place in a world flooded with tears.

BLINDING DARKNESS

The legendary Water Serpent, most sacred of symbols, passing into the hands of the next chosen ignited fireworks as it would for those who followed. Invoking the spirit of the monster Labbu bestowed blessings of mystical power upon the one knowing its name. Babylon's mythological snake, like the phoenix, would rise up from its own ashes to cross portals opening oceans of night galaxies. Heavens weighted to open with clarions of bright chorus. Serpent visions ceded from nature herself sang from tips of fire bird wings transforming mysteriously into impenetrable walls of water. The great Viper's mediation of both physical and spiritual worlds would erupt into star clusters as that of the Seven Sisters.

Under those primordial lights the castle stronghold would be transformed into a protector of this earth; keeping safe priceless artifacts resting within her halls amidst the bones of ancestors. Over centuries beings most incorporeal surrendered themselves willingly to await the succession of the Water Serpent's power. Entombed deep within the stones of the castle they accepted Imled as one of their own, chosen by the Chessman to wait.

The old player having been dealt what most would have shied from had not always been able to checkmate the Opponent's king. Accorded specific rulings the Chessman played to disable the woeful plight of living kind. What had challenged him gave him strength. This he would pass to the next. Skillful years engraved wisdom upon the wistfulness of youth; lines marking his passage through many lives to this sentry place. Creased was the fabric of his soul where many battles had been fought. Imled's love sustained him; laughter laced silken webs kissing the corners of his eyes.

Her dreams had seen her to the coming of ancient storms; the Pleiades sweeping across the skies. Powerful energies flooded the castle to waken those waiting within portrait frames. Imled had first known these beings as critical; their fixed gazes ciphering her every move. She came to accept them as examiners testing her knowledge and spirit as she learned the Chessman's practice; came to hold each of the artifacts they had brought to the castle.

Today their soft voices enveloped her like delicately woven silks; wisdom turning over as do leaves turn their backs before spring rains. Lining the walls at their feet, the objects held safe in curio cases glowed with the very light that had placed them to rest. Imled had learned the intrinsic parts they had played in unlocking the many secrets hidden within history. Fine pigmented strokes of oil paint layered their stories onto linen surfaces in animated testament to lives richly lived. She knew her story would one day be told as such for it seemed with each passing of expression the next in line of succession reached out to touch who followed here.

Symbols etched to the canvas backs told of how each of those caught by the artist had influenced history beyond the castle's gate. In a chair sat a Bedouin boy holding a shell shaped urn; desert sun catching the green of his kohl rimmed eyes, their light echoing those of a young woman in simple desert robes. In quiet unnamed strength she stood with her husband, ethereal hand raised in benediction. Their gift to the castle, a slate of petrified black shells curled as tightly as clustered rose buds, sparkled and danced on the coffered ceiling mirroring stars in the cloudless desert sky. A regal queen sat within her frame, a clairvoyant balancing the moon on her crown of braided tress.

A regal queen sat within her frame,
a clairvoyant
balancing the moon on her crown of braided tress.

Persia 1837; the Layth story continues ....

Silence drew breath from each unsure step. The Elder stopped, Layth tight to his side. Memories of mystical journeys on the back of a silvery white bird dissipated as they cautiously prepared to enter the village; secrets gathered from the hall of gods locked behind mute testament. The Elder leaned down, eyes motioning his grandson towards the furthest point of the narrow village street. Beneath a loosely hung canopy a group of men huddled shoulder to shoulder immersed in malice. From where they stood the Elder heard his name drift out from smoke filled shadows. Carried on the wisps of conversation was talk filled of drought, danger and threatened crops. Then came a thicker smoke curling with the stench of ruin rising slowly, inexorably, rolling from ferocious mouths. The old man's own prophesies, soiled by derision, were being fed out in acid drifts; a thousand tiny cuts folding back, eroding his place as Elder.

Layth recoiled from the heat building inside the shadow haze. He looked up to his grandfather who signaled him, cautioning in taut whisper, *"Be still."* Taking Layth's hand in a strong grasp, the Elder led their move towards the group under the canopy; forearmed to match what gathered against them. Ready to face that which had troubled him for years the old man dropped the pain he had carried to walk straighter into the twisted words of strangers.

Leaning down, *"Make no mention of the finding. The tangle we approach could strike heightened frustrations and anger into flames."* Lips pressed, Layth's nod was taut with need to protect the seal on the hill. Thoughts of the stone which lay waiting for them wove into his breath, touching beyond the firing excitement of his mind to a timeless well deep within. Here he saw the true shape of what he and his grandfather were to confront; an old darkness redefining its purpose.

Searching through the haze, he scanned the men who gathered, their voices colliding as worries tumbled into accusations. As they neared the group a dead silence fell to the canopy's underbelly, rising in sifting arrogance, swelling the cloth into the afternoon shade of an old tree. Exposed, the group rustled in discomfort; shame drawing the ghostly curtain around the group. Rifled talk billowed from the smoke curving around them in tremulous shapes of deadly scimitars, blades drawn across the shoulders of those who poisoned the village.

Layth followed his grandfather's lead into the gathering. The specter of severed heads rolling as warning could not bar the Elder from entering to find the help needed within the hold of tainted vapors.

The two went unnoticed as the strangers continued weaving lies and unformed truths; binding listeners. They spoke against the Elder and his teachers, not sensing the one they attacked was near; not seeing how he witnessed the spell of mistrust they wove nor did they remark as he spoke to his grandson. *"This is what I have often spoken of Layth. You have learned well the lessons of gathering fires. Innocence without conscience falls to subterfuge in the hands of those unconscious of reproach. Sham-faced, those responsible for deceit would bring harm to the world seeking only division in belief. They share no thoughts with those who teach Truth as Divine to all on earth. To stand as sentry against such thoughts is to stand watch against darkness."*

Since they had woken together on the shores of the dreamlands guarded by the hilltop palms, Layth had felt a greater bond with his grandfather. He knew his grandfather possessed of deep wisdom but since their journey to places unseen he could see that his grandfather looked beyond the material into the soul of humankind. Having crossed time and understanding journeying with his grandfather he had himself stepped into a greater strength and knowing. This way of thought would be his guide until he too reached for the stars.

Across the faces gathered, a familiarity of kinship was disturbed by something terribly wrong. Loud laughter roiled in the group with talk of hidden treasures, lost cities and fantasies told by story tellers. With thoughts of the stone holding him steady Layth's eyes traveled over those sitting until caught in the stare of the stranger who faced him through the dark. The eyes in their directness cut Layth to the core of his being with implacable hostility. Life pulsing from the hilltop dream seized when he saw one of the men twisted his fingertips ambitiously together; rings catching the light from shadow.

Layth froze, emotions bursting to flood images that crashed over his grandfather. The boy was stunned, deeply shaken. It was clear something had struck; shock leaving the boy breathless. His grandfather leaned down, *"What is the matter?"* he asked quietly. Eyes swelling with tears, Layth started again to breathe slowly. Whispering beneath drowning conversation continuing as if they were not there Layth explained, *"This is no ordinary sharing of stories Grandfather. This is an actual snake pit. Death hangs in the air as does the suffocating heat. "Those men ... Those men, I remember having seen in the past. Those men, they came to our house."*

The corners of Layth's mouth quivered; tightening his voice to whispers. The Elder blocked the boy from view of the gathering, squatting, he laid his hand on the boy's arm to steady him.

"Grandfather, when I was very small those two men came to our home. They shouldered the door, pushed into our house. Others were there too. Father offered them coin these men let spill to the floor. They held Father, struck Mother, kicking coin to walls. Shielding Mother, Father was pulled away by the attackers. Those two sitting there in the shadows beat him, tying his wrists through an endless roar of shouting. Father kept his eyes to watching Mother;

saying nothing. His expression frightened me for I had never seen such pain as in his silence. He held secrets; over and over, nothing more would be found he told them. Their rage grew; the men screamed louder throwing Father to the floor. Kicking him, they threatened Mother who wept from fright. I hid waiting for help to come but no one came."

"The shadow in the room, though it saved me became a blanket of shame for I could not save my parents. I stayed quiet wrapped in a shroud of dishonor. That man rubbed his finger tips as he does now; rings catching this day's light as they did the flame of the lamp that night. Behind the blazing rings, the man spoke words I could not understand. I wanted to run to Mother but did not. I crawled to the shadows along the edge of the wall then under the table on the other side of the room. I curled up, making myself small. Everything grew more horrible. Looking to the tall blue cupboard where I knew a loose plank on the bottom shelf was a door to safety, I crept towards it, crossing the threshold to push it aside and then climbed through. Mother had shown me this saying Father had hollowed a cave behind to be my home one day."

"Terrified, I watched breathless through a crack as the noise and yelling grew like a great storm. One of the men looked to me so sharply I feared having been found. To the back of the cave I thought I saw light. The tunnel covered me; swallowing me into the dark, like night it pushed away the noise. Mother had told me this cave would be safe for treasure. She said I was her treasure. This would be my safe place. How could she have known monsters would come, rob our lives, leaving me in the earth's belly behind the blue cupboard?"

"At the back of the cave I disappeared from myself. Under echoes of screaming the noise outside the cupboard was like thunder. I felt the oil lamp crash to the ground and heard its stone body rolling to the far wall. The front door slammed shut, silence growing so big it frightened me. Across the face of the cupboard, flames burst, engulfing our home in walls of fire. Thick smoke pushed its way deep inside the dugout blinding me with flickering ash. I could feel hands leaping towards the cupboard; grabbing everything, leaving in their wake nothing but skeletons and charred remains. Heat pushed past the loose plank, heaving it. Threats followed me deeper into the channel of the cave. I moved on until I could go no further, closing my eyes tightly, back turned on my parents thinking all was lost."

"My spine stiff to a wall of terror, I wanted to run but a mysterious grip on my neck held me with whispers of consoling comfort. Easing open my stinging lids, the faintest sliver of light blurred my vision. Something beyond the earth wrapped its cloak about me, wiping all memories away."

"I woke. I did not want to leave the earth. Your cries of rage led me to crawl out into the safety of your arms leaving behind the memories caught in the glitter of golden rings. Today the stranger's hand cuts free the past. In the smoke of these fires I am released of shame."

The maturity and wisdom he saw made the old man look at the boy in a different way. Taking Layth in a firm embrace, *"Why have you never spoken of this before?"*

"Mother told me I would not be able speak of this. What has been sundered from life for these long years, the world of demons, keyed by the power of sight has unlocked. Imprisoned, kept safe since that hate filled night, my world flooded with tears. These long years of silence spared me the madness of pain that would have consumed me. You took me from the fire, her spirit kept the fire from me. I have grown strong. I see these men. "

Pinching waves of smoke drew the old man to look with fierceness at the intent of those shadowed; vile motives cursing their every word.

The strangers continued spilling poison into the gathering of villagers unaware that the elder and his grandson stood but a few feet away. Ashen with grief, anger lashing out, he could see the strangers shift in their seats with discomfort as his fury met its mark. More than having destroyed his family that terrible night, it was the bloodless way they had returned, spreading more of their deadly venom. Knowing things could falter in the heat of rage he brought himself back from the years of pain to the imperative of this day.

"Stories of your survival, rumors that you were saved may have brought them here to the source to discover if indeed this was true. Do you think any one stranger might have thought you saved from the flames and thus with power could name their evil? We are endangered, threatened by forces seeking the unknown." His voice had steadied the boy enough to thrust him back into sudden memories. The strangers seemed blind to their presence.

"*They did not see me. Buried behind the blue cupboard, I heard whispers. This morning I woke from sleep, hearing whispers calling me to walk the desert. Was I led to the stone on the hilltop? We are not as before. We have seen the world of Ancients. I feel their strength growing around us; arms of gods sheltering our every move. Our lives will not continue as we have known. These men are here and for good reason. Evil would not have returned this day to our village if not for the stone. We have touched that which is alive, felt travelers of mystical paths. If this is what Mother and Father protected no harm will come to us.*"

"*Look into the faces of these men, what they embody makes me seethe with anger. They destroyed life and yet return bringing further deceptions. No longer that terrified four year old boy, I will confront them. Death will rise from within the ashes they left to desert winds. What they had consumed by violence will guide me.*"

Spirit's hand reached out of the smoke to rest on his shoulder; brushing the rage that gathered about him. "*Storms of violence, misguided thoughts, make no sense to futures be they towards others, to the earth herself. Trust my words Layth. Hear what I say, obey those from the Silence for they hold the key to what manifests.*" Layth followed the soothing voice which slipped away before he realized its source, a voice he knew before his own heartbeat.

*"Evil would not have returned this day to our village,
if not for the stone."*

His grandfather cut across time to bring him back to their path and the village. *"This is what we will do; speak only when spoken to, giving simple answers only when asked. Speak only to our people. We will ask for help gathering of flock. Say nothing of water. Masked creatures hide in shadows about us. I hold the precious nature of your find be kept as sacred. Disclosure to disbelievers would anger those from the Silence who have guided us this day, have led us here. Let us move without fear into this danger."*

The two walked with purpose towards the gathering. The strangers looked in their direction; dark eyes seeming to take no notice. Turning their gaze back to the men gathered beneath the canopy, they continued their inquisition of the tales told at village gathering fires.

When the villagers turned their own thoughts to water and village worries the strangers caught the discussion, bringing it back to the ancient stories filled with myth and mysteries.

There were brothers who stood at the edge of the group. These the Elder had thought to be strong, of reliable character. The younger often questioned the guidance of elders but having known the boy from birth had seen his heart was sound. Without acknowledging the strangers he asked the brothers for help and they agreed; respect silencing any questions. While his grandfather spoke with the boys Layth found himself fixated, staring at the strangers. Anger made him forget caution. Hair on the back of his neck rose one at a time. The spirit voice returned in a wisp of scented spice.

Its loving caress steadied the boy in reassurance almost forgotten. "*My son, the wisdom of what must be done is greater than can be seen. I promised you that day would come ordained by ancient reason. It approaches. Trust those of the Silence for they will share with you as they have guided me these long years with secrets of All Ages. Patience, renew strength knowing we are here. Your father and I are next to you as promised. Assisted by us you shall find the answers to that night long ago. It was necessary change wrought upon our lives. Remember the sliver of light that touched you in the cave your father opened for you behind the blue cupboard. It greets you again carrying wonders beyond imagination*". The talk from the group of men seemed to grow louder and fraught. Layth drew back into his anger but the soft voice called his heart again.

"*Child back away, well away. This is not of your concern. They cannot see nor hear those of our lineage. You and your grandfather remain safe. Only the brothers can see you. Take them and leave, leave now*".

Layth felt the strength of peace fill his limbs. He would leave these strangers to be taken through their own greed by those of kind; this better than his own revenge on these damaged souls. "*Justice is done,*" slipped under Layth's breath. His grandfather questioned. "*It was but simple reverie, Grandfather.*"

With acquiescence ordained, two brothers freed themselves from smoky shadows drifting, to follow Layth and his grandfather along the path towards their service to the Silence. The strangers did not remark on their leaving.

The Stone of Ea
Chapter VI

Chapter Six
The Stone of Ea

The Castle on the Hill

The great corridors had followed Imled for years sharing each threshold passed in the joy reflected gaze of eyes unchained, settled behind lids of crystal caskets. In vastness of her new life she took comfort in the walls unchanging and so stopped to inquire an empty space come to surface shadowed in timbre; the beat of her step forever changed.

The wall had grown; wood grains separating into dustless crevices. Somber joints snaked into tiny threads of silver strings; serpentine kisses licking the panel surface suffused with moon-like beams crisscrossing one another to the edges of the newly formed encasement.

Imled blinked in disbelief to the manifestation of an ancient crystal skull floating in the nascent alcove; jaw dislodged as if to speak. A child of Yucatan, her homeland veined with sacrificial wells, she had touched this exquisite form of Maya origin; knowing this artifact an omen of death and life.

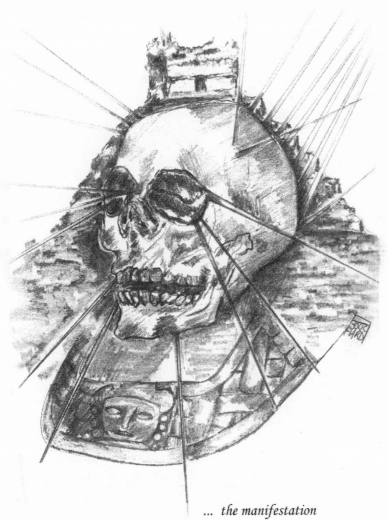

... the manifestation
of an ancient crystal skull
floating in the nascent alcove;
jaw dislodged as if to speak ...

When she reached out, the vision eluded her touch, melting away, pouring into liquid reflection which mirrored her face in a clear blue surface, the pool changing shape from water to blood. Brimming with tears her soul swam oceans spirited by the tips of ancients' fingers breaking the surface of mind; diving into the brilliance of ancestors.

She knew prophet oracles manifest, having seen vivid projections carved in sacred *Cenotes* of Mexico cupping waters ritually to join the Chessman's castle, this great stone vessel sailing on waves to the strange moment when she happened upon a tall foreigner that studied her ancestral Pyramids; causing life's transformation.

Such a well as this was crafted by power to carry souls. Would this aqueous chamber in the wall be the resting place for her heart, her other, the Chessman? Devotion filled her eyes, escaping into liquid terms of endearment, protesting what she understood to be inevitable.

Imled stood motionless afraid of separation, so fragile she could not yet feel how the delicate disciplines escaping the new extension would take her into strength; communion with the castle as its master. Sewn within fine wood grains and knots clear of dust were spirits initiated by the grand design protecting the hope of humankind; precious initiates laid within crystal gathering their will, calling one of their caste to wear the crown of prophesy.

At hall's end, from inside a mist suspended over the carpet running, the heiress appeared in spectral egress cloaked in transparent silken gauze, jeweled headdress holding pearls, each containing a tapestry of one life lived; lustrous visions held in silvered plumes of iridescence curling about the air like translucent tendril fingers. Eyes of aquamarine reflecting memories in ghostly expression, the duchess held in abeyance the past to greet the future; slipping back into her portrait lit by ancestral eyes the color of water.

In the center in his bed carved of rich scented wood, the Chessman listened with care to silver threads projecting onto the canopy's screen; gems of a rich life. The air filled with unforgettable textures of a simpler life where unlocked doors, unbarred windows kept safe a home. He closed his eyes caught to the sudden marinade of delicate garden scents traveling the dewed wingtips of robins; berries mixed with perfumes of lilac and spring roses welcoming new morn.

The Chessman communed in a vulnerability satiated with compassion and wisdom; each day since his investiture in the castle spent carefully gathering signs and portents of the great wave that would wash over the low areas of human existence; the new Golden Age ordained before time that would arrive on the mark of his long life. He had cautioned Imled that animating forces would soften closed lids to break the seal, raising from deep beneath the gardens those cradled in crystal stasis who watched from painted eyes set deep into castle halls. Signaling humankind of their arrival Divine teachers most needed to restore troubled worlds would allow permit; reconnecting with those of the portraits to reach through silence resurrected.

Warmth pumped from the castle's heart, flushing through Imled's veins; memories of initiates who had gone before, anointing her, filling the vital space surrounding with principled forces. What had expressed itself this day was simple truth of how these devotees through sorrow helped key reason against the blindness of humankind over millennia; elementals crucial to the survival of Great Mother Earth ignored, outlawed, leaving her vulnerable to destruction.

A brumous ray of light crossed the melancholic passage to mark the end to Imled's journey, entrance to the old man's chambers glowing with the Northern Lights of his childhood; last of the visuals spun onto his canopy by the dream catcher.

Rippling folds of joy and sorrow irrevocably entwined with tears to welcome decree by societies most secret; transformation of her life for his.

... jeweled headdress holding pearls,
each containing a tapestry of one life lived;
lustrous visions held
in silvered plumes of iridescence curling about the air
like translucent tendril fingers ...

Persia 1837; the Layth story continues ....

Having left oppression trapped in the mist beneath the canopy the four gave one another support, twisting their way from village to travel where at the base of the hill the Elder risked to forewarn the brothers of that which could meet them on the path. The boys continued through his warnings with thoughts riding the peerless import of youth's concerns.

Impossible to share what had been encountered by Layth and himself he felt best pressing on, his slow pace supported by the crooked old stick he had plucked from a pile of dried woods thrown off to the path's side. The Elder saying little, his staff firmly gripped in gnarled hand, resolved to dreadful waves of sun's fire reflecting from the sands, led the group up towards the hilltop; boys following behind under the last rays of the punishing sun.

The blistering heat that had earlier sprung from the earth to plague Layth and his grandfather escaped to surface the path shifting beneath their feet; crumbling earth defying each step the four took towards the stand of palms. Treacheries of this incline were unforgettable for him; countless times since his youth he had traveled this way, chafed under the unspoken blame of the land. At his heels the boys covering their mouths, fraught with choking, fought to breathe through the dust heaving up from the unquiet rumbling of sandaled feet.

Impatience born of nervous apprehension fed Layth the need to push past, run ahead of his grandfather and the others. Held to trust in his stride kept steady by the Elder's pace, he drew the brothers on, footsteps echoing tight to his back, without matter to issue. Eyes to the ground, the four watched compromised feet disappear in the dust of stones rattling the slope, breaking away from sandals to rise dancing into a wall of tiny earth particles feinting desolation at the hill top; wispy images of old palms drawn closer into view.

Over what was thought to be the last obstacle, they crossed; met by a chilling breeze filled with the eerie presence of salt filled air. The brothers postured from the unexpected assault on sense; sharp sounds of dried grasses pinching ankles, snapping at sandal straps. Invisible force sought to fire the toll of heat; startling expectations snaking up legs to impress upon confusion; keeping from them the life of new green swaying atop palm stalks that bowed in reverence to Layth and his grandfather. In deference, the old man acknowledging the miracle swept his arm out from under his cloak, signaling Layth to reclaim the staff that swayed in passing breezes, standing to mark what they had so carefully dressed that morning against loss to sudden changes wrought by prevailing powers. Concealed beneath desert remains, secured from being discovered by intruders, the find had survived the wait until their return. Layth running past his grandfather stopped abruptly to pull the staff from where he had placed it earlier to the side of the mound of stick and straw, releasing built up sands to quickly shift, filling in the depression of the pole's tip. Collapsing to his knees he reached for the edge of his head's wrap, removing the cloth to tightly wind it about his hand against razor-bites of debris. At first touch the straw trembled in resolve, the sands respondent, pushing off into sinuous waves that stretched magically across the desert ridges; keying call for ritual unseen. A wind emerged furious from surrounding dunes, sweeping into giant hands, cupping the group readied for trial.

Layth thrown to the stone in threat of violence felt the challenge, his lion heart stalwart, head whirling in calls of voices from dreams, the stone exposed; village boys huddling in fear to the sudden violence of nature. As the vortex drained sands from the grounds they grabbed at one another terrified of being swallowed by the eroding desert. Eyes closed tight to pending doom they did not see the revelation of the ancient granite stone.

Uneasy with their reaction, sensing crisis in the boys, the Elder took to task his authority, stepping in to deliver them from any further damaging. *"Something of very great importance manifests in this place. I am confident we have been led here to meet a greater destiny; water. Loosen hold on this lack of understanding of yours, stay calm, for the ancients speak mysteriously from depressions hollowed deep beneath these sands. You both will come to see as Layth and I this glistening stone holds a message carved long ago in*

ancient script by those who having passed this way did so with infinite knowledge.
Must be we have gathered here by direction of those who breathe life to dreams.
Make haste, remove the stone lid, night flies as do days; I feel its descent."

Layth and the brothers looked to the sky blinded by
the sun cresting the old man rendered holy by this immersion into
flame; rites readying them to follow his every command.

The Elder motioned them to position around the edge
of the enactment whose dome answered in reflection, sparkling like a
large jewel in the settling sun. They placed themselves to combine
strengths around the circle, ambition avid to unveil what secrets could
be concealed, hidden from adventurous eyes. Fingertips sifting sand
to the resistance of the granite's edge they waited the Elder's count,
pearls of sweat gathered, spewing to creased brows. On the third
count of the Elder's staff, the three tugged and pulled to the beat of
inhalation, hearts called by mystery, eyes closed tightly against effort,
fighting the stone with a relentlessness none could have storied. The
hands of Ea reached out from the Silence, unseen, radiating beams of
light from what had been etched to granite surface of the seal.

Within his blindness, the Elder saw the cuneiform
inscriptions as portal to the Earth's bound secrets; a key encrypted to
a world that would not allow passage to buried chambers. Images of
Layth astride the silver white bird flooded his mind; soaring through
skies of Babylon the realization his grandson could key the future.

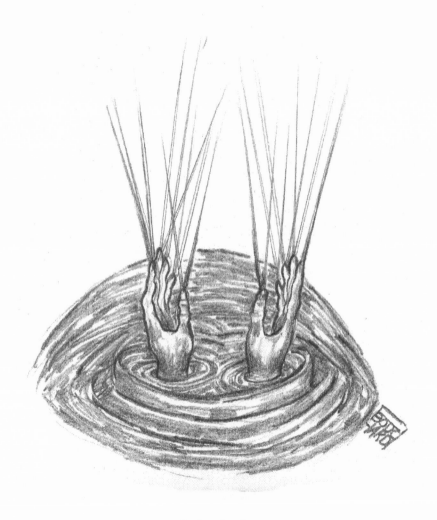

The hands of Ea
reached out from the Silence, unseen,
radiating beams of light...

Failing to breach ancient rule, the others gathered, preparing themselves once more, applying pressure to legend, prying at the lid's edges over and over. Unrelenting, the stone simply would not budge, no matter how they shifted themselves, moved positions, strained themselves until exhaustion; pulling until they sat one after the other; collapsed, feet ground into dune sands. Defeated, each sank into their own, emptiness creeping into the stalks of waving palms that held vigil over failure.

The eye of the stone turned, watching from its strong hold, reposed to act beyond lingering doubt, tentative movement sounding its decision to accept the judgment of the wind.

Flexed against the stiffness of centuries its surface twisted to struggle from the desert's embrace; shudders yielding under loud cracking. What ancient wisdom had sealed for centuries began to offer of itself; light pulsing into the air from under cover, exhaling stale sweet scent in greeting to those who had awakened her. Joyous freedom swelled their robes about the four like billowing sails of tall ships, shaking them who leaned away from her kiss as if to run, only to be left staring near incapable of movement.

Lips quivered as did the lid that pivoted its insert; streaming tears from wide eyes as the stone broke its place of rest.

Beneath the crevasse, threadlike cracks releasing a perfume of temple incense unprecedented turned to passing desert winds, fusing the shrill whistles of captured souls funneled in windstorms wildly rushing past the four; bodies captive by the onslaught of divine intrigue. The attack left the brothers senseless, gripped by a paralyzing fear that shook them, seizing their limbs, numbing them to speech, cowering before the Elder who lay hand to knowledge of ancient mysteries.

"This sensation is of the ordinary; alchemy of temple dwellers drawing outsiders to this sacred place, a land flowing with the many stories carried by four winds across seas. We have been chained, drugged to follow the secrets of the Laws of the Circle. Those no longer having human shape have come here from parallel worlds; giving us reasons profound to strike open the sands with promise of further life." The Elder communed with every line bestowed upon his expression, as the unmovable slowly began to wheel at their feet; turning over, grinding into disturbing sounds of deep thunders.

Moving clockwise then countering until it ground with an even more powerful surge of air that hissed like a bed of snakes pitting more tiny cracks into the granite's mortar as it pulsed from its place of resting. The stone loosened, gently rising up feather-like as would palm branches caught in a breeze, hanging above their heads momentarily, dropped to strike the earth under its true weight with a deafening thud on a soft nearby dune. Crystals of fresh blown sand folded in, burying the sinking cap that suddenly reappeared thrusting a huge mushroom of loose material that billowed high darkening the afternoon skies.

Overturning clouds clashed, moaning like muffled wagging tongues wakening into waves of ancient conformance carried off by passing winds. Centered within cries of sacrilege for this defilement storming skies proclaimed the unimaginable, *"This place wherein Truth immemorial dwells holds captive those judged by the wind; voices twining dimensions around you, spinning unheard seventh notes."*

First to re-enter mind, body and spirit facing a silence of intervals remaining was the Elder released from forces unrelenting.

"We bear witness to that which has been freed from this land, voices imprisoned; lost to cities buried by the power of these sands. We have been marked so never to reveal that which has been decreed as our trust. Power is sweet to those unfaithful; alchemy intoxicating as rotting fruit which in its spell destroys the perfection of hummingbird flight. Not only Truth is active here. Proceed with caution."

He studied the boys, careful they may have pulled away from his words; wanting to run from this place, to push on others the fears constricting their temples. He knew their minds, crafting challenge to draw them back to purpose.

"Understand that most will disclaim what you say as nonsense. Run you might, to find no option for the choice in this matter is not now for any of us; stay you must to help through events unexpected and beyond reasoning. From beneath the sands is clearly spoken, unbelievers will be afflicted, left without speech in protection of this sacred space. Rest assured we are led; through all we will be within watch of those most treasured."

His voice dropped under the weight of silence, eyes shifting, arms raised with palms open to receive the benefice of the air; vanquished symbols fulfilling grace. Speech left village timbre to mine a vein none but the elder could see.

"Carried to us unheard on desert winds for thousands of years history escapes from hollowed darkness this day. Those from the Silence will again take flight into human form becoming travelers in possession of divine learning and expression. They poise to blind sight, take speech, silence hearing of those who would summon harm to prophesies rising from the ashes of all worlds."

"I serve primordial purpose since having stepped upon this hill's top but to what intent I am left to interpret. This place of prevalence, a sacred union of all responses proclaimed by those of like spirit whose voices circle planets, expands the sense of the right and the wrong for those who resonate of same resolve. All must return light unto day for in time they will consume those of untrue hearts determined to keep our daughters and sons from eternity."

*"We bear witness
to that which has been freed from this land,
voices imprisoned;
lost to cities buried by the power of these sands."*

In trance, the old man's words seemed to demonize what they had witnessed escaping the granite seal. Layth winced, thinking to intercept the messenger; lips parting to break the spell stilling as his grandfather continued to speak through universal counsel.

"Let it be known Life must change anon. Lateral worlds have referenced desert winds where thwarted goals of ancients have once again reached out into the heart of those silenced. That which exists in all dimensions will determine the outcome of humankind; exacted to the rules of nature's auspices."

The Elder slipped off the stream of prophecy; altered by ashes of faith he sank into his robes, shuddering at his own humanity caught into youth's vitality. Not knowing what response required of them the boys had withdrawn in witness to the old man's flight, springing through fear to catch his fall. Emptiness collapsed, thought freed. *"I have held the core of silence, looked through a ribbon of glass into a gift so fragile, beautiful, with the capacity to draw blood from us all in the future. What lies at the edge of our universe is the well binding all creation; source holding ultimate control capable of rendering into nothingness lines the mind of man has scratched into a parched earth; fragmenting creation; demonizing holy spirit."*

"Should we not appreciate our differences? Every tear reflects in its own way, mirroring a place or point in someone's life. Be they of laughter or pain, the source is human kindness celebrated both entering and passing; air, earth,

fire and water becoming as one in the fifth. With all elements in place, the way is clear. Behind each mask is the human heart as yet undistorted by custom and the cathexis of power. Let us continue our part in bringing this darkness to air before the sun leaves us." He moved to the tunnel's mouth; boys gathering around to peer into the small lightless void; only one among them with both form and courage to slip into that darkness.

The Elder raised his arm to rest upon Layth's shoulder, *"I trust you to this place of divine vision and those long past worlds but I fear the human part you are called to play, my greatest treasure."*

"Grandfather, I have no fear of what lies in the darkness beyond the opening if here we find the fifth element of which you have spoken. It will bridge space between souls and heavenly bodies bringing humanity peace; a serenity never felt dispels what fear may have awaited me within this lightless abyss." Layth's voice carried strength in a quiet of new found wisdom.

His grandfather cautioned, *"This space is unlike any other. Granite stone has tipped open an unending secret confiding to your lion's heart to trust the sacredness of histories channeled through me this day from inside the narrow pathway. Leading deep into the earth, its extent invisible, this hollow may be the beginning of something wanting; more than we are able to comply with."*

*"I trust you to this place of divine vision
and those long past worlds
but I fear the human part you are called to play,
my greatest treasure."*

The taller of the two brothers pushed forward, words falling from impatient lips. *"You speak of elements, such things as my brother and I know nothing of. Confused banters steer us away from our purpose, taking us quickly into night, stealing our light. Why do we not take our chances simply entering the tunnel? Twisted talk is but fantasy when water is what we should be looking for, our need of water, nothing more or my brother and I take leave".* Nodding to threat, the other boy too, felt happiest thinking matters to be as clear as the need for water; mysterious winds and unclaimed voices best forgotten.

The old man looked through the boys staking their measure, turning attentions to the youngest of the brothers, laying hands on the boy's shoulders; speaking directly into questioning eyes. *"The only one small enough to enter the passageway is Layth who must rest if he is to successfully descend within the hollow. Our part to play is to make certain he is kept safe during his descent."*

"You are to collect our needs which upon entering my house you will find; a lamp sitting by the doorway, fire sticks and to the back of the painted cupboard, bundled rope. Great care must be taken for none must find of our work this day. Traveling eyes must not see you enter or leave. Those men from beneath the canopy would mercilessly press questions upon you, answer to nothing, take leave, you have come retrieving something lost as you tended sheep."

"Demon minds bent by greed, stained with suspicion, blight the very air we breathe. Leave us now. Pray Allah keeps you concealed, able to detect

what messengers of untruth pace amongst us."

In the way of boys, he found the Elder's words to be compelling; engaging with adventure to be met, the boy nodding with the excitement of youth. *"I will do as you say, protecting us from danger. That I promise. I promise."* The boy turned away to run as fast as his feet would carry him. To the steep of the pathway he dropped from sight disappearing in a blinding cloud of fiery dust not unlike the ball that had rolled furiously down the hill carrying Layth within its belly. When it was clear they had taken to task the Elder smiled knowing the joy that carried that young man as it had so seeded his grandson seemingly long ago. He would be safe. *"We wait,"* he said looking over to the others, *"We run with him sheltered from harm within the spirit of the earth."*

Feeling a wave of disturbance pass through the grounds beneath him, the elder readied for what unraveled, growing in strength, shaking loose bits of dried grass, sticks and pebbles to flood his sandals. In a hail of thunder the granite stone wheeled, snaking in broad curves, dragging itself over to seal again the tunnel which had been exposed, settling itself into the opening with the gentle sigh of voices caught in folds of blown silks brushing strings of ephemeral lyres.

"Take heed, rest children," a passing breeze whispered, *"Approaching this place are those of lesser consciousness. Beneath this sandy slope*

we lift you will hide yourselves as we blind sight of these intruders." Furtive words sweeping a hollowed bed within the dune bade the Elder take his grandson and the taller boy leading them to the sandy embankment soon to find themselves buried beneath a blanket of broken twigs and palm bits. Outside the cover, quiet fell.

To the bottom of the hill's path the round mass of dust burst forward; spilling the charging boy into the old sun bleached courtyard.

Shaking off the dust gathered in his clothes he slipped into the old man's house quite assured not a soul had witnessed his return; assurance shattered with approaching voices, drawing him from his cause to a casement window in dread of specters; dust clad silhouettes. The close distance approach of the strangers dropped him to the floor

Fearing his presence uncovered, the boy hid in hope they would continue past, leaving him to the particles of dust that stirred into a wall of protection as promised by the voices in the wind.

... the round mass of dust burst forward;
        spilling the charging boy
                into the old sun bleached courtyard.

Flame on the Hilltop
Chapter VII

Chapter Seven
Flame on the Hilltop

The Castle on the Hill

Portrait alcoves leading up to the newly formed recess contained single-minded purpose; lives given in reservation of right to disseminate secrets guarded; mantic powers lending themselves to stairs of aquamarine. Emptiness heaved ominous within the initiate's chest, responsibilities searching from within the filaments spun of Persian desert stories; grains of cities buried in sin. Through this pained abrasion of ancient frenzy Imled was held captive but she found safety under streams of crystal blue expression that poured over her and in trust that the gathering of Whippet hounds approaching would, without question, lift her spirit. Quickly they turned about her, caressing shoulders brushing fingertips, non-judging airs like those of adoring children, innocence snuggling to fit into the fullness of her skirt folds; giggles spilling to the portraits, granting breath long held in confinement escape from canvas frame edges ....

"Let us see what the spider has caught in its web from boyhood memories. Monitor, display what has been eluded for decades, the blink of mind's eye eclipsed by old age."

Above the fireplace, projection secured itself with the distinct sound of tall rubber Billy boots whose loose wobbles sounded impatience in a run for Mr. Johnson's truck as it pulled up to the train station platform.

"I hated that sound." The Chessman remembered to problems manifest during untimely spring floods and how travels by open back vehicles measured strength as children fought others for foot dangle space. Nearly every year the maundering creek at the foot of the hill grumbled, flowing over its banks, rusting the train tracks, rushing to join the lake. Old bridges disappearing beneath murky flood waters made the trek back and forth to distant schools treacherous, near impossible, but there was always someone to depend on with an open back truck to rescue when the big yellow bus, its bottom step submerged, stalled, refusing to pick up those waiting from the train's platform; Zorro lunch pails nervously scratched with graffiti tied up with old weathered leather belts, books and notepads bundled against the rain, all clutched to chests snapped under plastic raincoats.

The Chessman stood crooked, smiling by the reminder of one day early his seventh August when he and his three siblings sat around the dining room table choosing from a Sears catalogue; September being the start of school and end of berry bushes.

... the distinct sound of tall rubber Billy boots ...

On the floor above, at the point where the red wood banister pulled from the wall sat a closet smelling lightly of mothballs brimming with hand-him-downs, enough to last the next few lifetimes; his brothers planning his wardrobe for the forthcoming school years.

The Chessman felt the little boy's sadness; expression shorted, bowing to the logic of previously worn clothing handed down from older brothers rapidly growing, he holding to trust that his mother or grandmother would give him a reassuring nod that something crisp of his own, new, would be ordered in to see him through to the first days of school. Calendars passing through years to the edge of high school found everyone huddled again in ritual when a short sleeved shirt on a far page caught his interest. Grandmother Alice watched bright eyes widening under brows raised in a quiet hope, his neck extended, curious for something quite beautiful in blue plaid cotton. She smiled broadly gazing up at the Tiffany lamp that spilled its light through brass beveled green diamonds to the table's top. He had seen that familiar smile many times before, crinkled corners set in thought that something unexpected would join the other articles carried by the postman along the wooden sidewalk to be propped between the rickety doors of home. *"I miss you dearest Grandmama. Soft lines carved in the alabaster white of your face, colorless as death itself, cold to the touch warming the stages of my early life with courage to carry me to this final chapter."*

Over the long years he had never forgotten her, clinging to the few words she spoke to him last, memory of an unusually warm November's day and how her voice cracked to tears cutting the powder she so carefully applied to cover the years of guilt; her secrets hidden within a numbered marker, zipped away in the compartment of a small black purse leaning against the wall to the back of a closet shelf.

As Mr. Johnson's truck slowly backed up to the train's platform, the boy anxiously held firm to his place to secure a dangling spot at the truck's bed back. Toes gripping to the boots' insides, he managed to avoid mama's anger, feet cutting ridges in the murky creek waters. Unforgiving had the shallow twisting streams become to run along the train tracks. Overflowing they joined the threat of melting ice pouring down from the hilltop, flooding lake water erasing miles of populated roads with angry currents that swirled in wild undertow. The last five to board the rough slivering planks that lifted, pinching bottoms, laughed out loud. Those who had climbed on before cried with excitement. Fingertips hanging down as low as could be the children reached to carve their impression into the muddied mirrored reflections of red leafless dogwood branches caught in the lifeless opacity that rushed the truck's wheels.

It was one day in the many to follow, with the sudden loss of one of his boots, that a new thought triggered revelations causing him to look up at the incomprehensibility of this relentless flooding and the devastatingly painful effect it must have had on those not lucky enough to live on the neighboring hilltop.

As Mr. Johnston's truck wound magically round the many potholes the cresting waters had dug out of the asphalt road the Chessman mourned his loss as his boot rose one last time to sink beneath the waves. Soon the waters would pull back and simpler life would emerge from the water soaked soil leaving the townspeople to return, walk on the rails of the train tracks past the second set of rocks to pick sweet wild blueberries and mushrooms grown out of the mired northern lands.

Later it was floods of war that ravaged this world he loved; frustrated voices inside cries of pain unable to confront guilt turning into anger. The meaning of life for the Chessman was not as it should be; elements of extremism painting endless destruction with leaden justification, rending the middle way into unbreachable chasm. A life's time passed through such sorrow had brought him to this day most reckoned through an existence lived apart from others; endless questioning of the world preceding, histories of humankind.

"Oceans of tears from distant lands have found their way to near shores, spilling themselves across boundaries on their insatiable path, harming innocence of both other and their own; wisdom of Divine Order turned upon itself; foreigners in the lands beyond Egypt blinded to the love of neighbor. Time will alter

what has been woven. The choice of two paths, one of life and one of death will be made, and Life will be chosen; to love the Divine as foundation of all upon which to love neighbor in action and being, accepting neighbor as self."

Opened to dreams and ancient prophesy, guided to understand promise of a New Golden Age, he saw powerlessness supplant old orders, asserting the new. Power and creed believed undeniable would be overturned by simple Truth revealing lessons discovered by the Bedouin boy; revelations found deep beneath living roots of dead palms ....

Looking from the dogs into the depths of portrait souls, Imled was drawn for the first time to see through expressions of the collective; physical threads weaving colorless shades of sky into symbols pregnant with the element all shared. Enigmatic eyes held unrequited pain lost to saltwater pools of the most precious delicate lace; glass strings of the heart veining her own wound drawing her into association. Love lost, taken from youth that would never return, had scored sadness deep into the canvas faces; flawlessly paned.

Pulling back, bracing herself to the arm of the Caretaker's Chair, settled with intent as viewing gallery for study of the art crowning the glass curio cases, positioned by those stirring beneath the gardens to receive Imled in the wake of her dawning.

Ancestral records filled senses with the delicate play of liquid blue streaming from the jewels of the duchess. Closing her eyes, Imled could see what the Duchess so desperately clung to in the fisted folds of her skirts; behind lavish velvets, embroidered tears of lost love gathering in delicate silks sewn by years of brushing pain to side.

To her left was the Bedouin boy; kohl-rimmed eyes isolated in pinpoint reflections of sorrow she recognized; a constant companion from her decision to take up this journey of the Chessmen. To her right, a young man sported a cravat of French silk framing a pale visage steeped in drowned emotion; heart frozen soft, still awkwardly dealing with the unsinkable guilt for years lived with his parents held captive to an ocean's graveyard. The jeweled right hand of the magus Essitam held a ring Imled knew well, his left a cylinder of mystery; piercing eyes holding knowledge of a power yet greater than both. All had, as had she, unfulfilled love, hearts so fragile they would give unconditionally of their lives that others might survive.

"A new period in humankind's evaluation comes soon to rise making way for the ultimate demise of those who would force their beliefs upon innocents. Tyranny of our world through subversion of heart, mind and spirit will have an end to its abominations. Truth will prevail, leading the meek to survive."

*... Imled could see
what the Duchess
so desperately clung to
in the fisted folds of her skirts ...*

To the end of the hall beyond ancient oak, surrounded by dreams and those past, the Chessman quietly by himself, his soul still to this world, walked to the sudden rippled movement of silken bedding, its inhabitant surfacing, *"Have you tended the garden this morning?"* Maximus lunging himself from beneath the weight of the blankets, dropped to the mattress chewing the doll of the little Duchess. Letting go of the toy's foot, nose to the air, he looked past the door to Imled circling with the unerring purpose of a butterfly, soul tipping ephemeral wings, her spirit soaring into the heart of the castle's lofty grey expansions as had the Chessman's before her.

In succumbing to the inspiration of her teacher's way, her rebirth keyed the ultimate secret the gardens embodied; farewells sung into the history of the castle, recording time set in crystal caskets to be released by her hand wielding what the Chessman carried in the golden signet casement ring about his neck. *"Given new to the ways of the Order most secreted, my Caretaker, we bestow upon you that which I hold here to my fingers' tip, the key to millennia opening for you more than merely the rich tales of a boy."*

The Chessman's words echoing in memory, Imled stood to continue on her path; dampness of her shoes still squeaking, high pitches protesting the roughness of the carpet's threadbare weave worn by the years of door openings, closings, comings and goings.

"... we bestow upon you that which I hold here to my fingers' tip;
the key to millennia ..."

As she reached to insert her hand into the narrow crack between the Chessman's door and its oak frame, a flash blinding the darkness of the wood to colorless grain pivoted her to a dimension of swirling orbs carrying faces in fire.

Imled whirled in amazement to the brilliance of these prophesies set in bezels of flame; a lion's face, mane afire, bringing the Persian son to life in the fullness of the hall, burning away translucent painted masks revealing a myriad of symbols. Buried beneath thin lined gutters of delicate brush strokes were the cartographers' legend to blood lines established over centuries. More than relation by blue blood, those preserved by artist craft embodied one spirit of sanctity; nourished by sibylline societies. These impressions of meaning invisible to the eye yet traceable by finger's tip could only have been deciphered by one sustaining faith in a world sometimes godless; Imled now of their number.

The Initiate had often questioned why these figures lining the castle hallway moved her so but evidence had brought understanding. Each had been seared in the bond of soul wounded as her own had been by the wrenching loss of love's foundation. In her pain, fear had closed her sight to the brilliance alive around her. Initiation by fire had lit her eyes to the artifacts coiled beneath glass; glistening with reason.

This moment of revelation opened a space in time through which appeared a ghostly figure. To the furthest east facing wall at the hall's end, as bright as the rise of the morning sun an evocatively delicate female form slipped from an old tapestry, tipping toe towards her, iridescent weightlessness presenting itself in this creature dancing a narrow passage; airy silken ribbons aglow about her transparency; haunting whispery voices spilling from the tips of each tendril, beaming stars into glistening pearls throughout the castle, off into the distance.

The crowning shield atop her head glowed in filaments of images, spellbinding projections of wonders of the world filling the air; crystal and pearl forming light of shape and sound that dizzied sight before slipping back into an alcove. Freed of the spell Imled followed to the place of vision where touching her fingertips to a plaque mounted on the picture's frame she read *"Duchess Lady Laura Bennington"*. Lifting her gaze to meet that of the Duchess, Imled was amazed to find that the entire of the portrait had changed its face for the Duchess having stood the years alone, her paleness of alabaster framed in diaphanous silks, now held hand to the form of a small dog that looked at the Caretaker with the eyes of the Chessman's hound.......

Paused in the pale of morning light, the Chessman's eyes of aquamarine crinkled in delight from inside the shimmering feather tips of his millstone collar; he reaching through time with loving touches to the key essence of spirit.

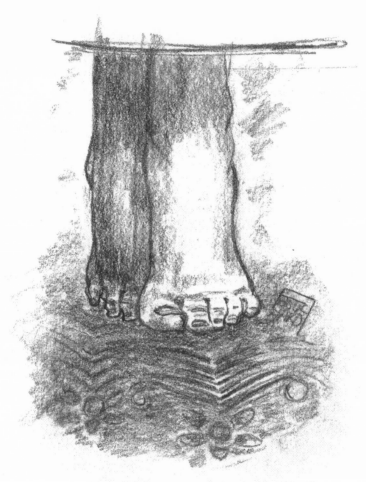

... female form slipped from an old tapestry,
tipping toe towards her,
iridescent weightlessness presenting itself ...

Persia 1837; the Layth story continues ….

The boy stopped breathing, a silent deathly sensation free falling from his still frozen courage to the souls of his sandals. A rhythm trembled; nervously pulsing blood jailed behind ribs, echoing panic into a heart enslaved to phantom voices of the hilltop, his Elder's warning pounding in his thoughts. *"Pray Allah keeps you concealed, able to detect what messengers of untruth pace amongst us."* His body shook with uncontrollable fear.

Huddling below the window's ledge, barred from discovery under the protection of the crooked shutters, drawing on the strength he possessed, the boy's unrelenting curiosity attracted him to a small opening which years of neglect had scraped into the wooden slats. He searched the shadows making their dark way past the Elder's house.

It was these men who had earlier approached the villagers with apparent interest in the heaviness of drought but now clearly concerned themselves with matters other than much needed water. Subsequently what they had entered engagement with, talks of common faith, eventually turned to words visiting ancient burial sites, crypts, then finally onto treasures that might embody powers supernatural.

*"the boy's unrelenting curiosity
attracted him to a small opening
which years of neglect
had scraped into the wooden slats."*

Thoughts spun out within questions before splaying to answers, clever knowledge of Bedouin hills and surrounding lands entertaining those gathered under the canopy to sight relief from relentless dread. Play of chatter swung in the air like blades silver of smoke, actively cutting down suspicion as it rose to meet their demands for stories bound to rituals. Charm swathed in palm blood drew out answers staining riddles meant only for the cover of gathering fire nights.

Treacherous intent hovering in the mist had not breached the safety of the Elder's house; offering the boy a small respite into which memory seeped. Braced in this moment under the window he remembered sly telling of those who had wrenched ancient beauty from the deep of the sand only to be taken with their stolen treasures; foreign cleverness banished to the depths of the rivers Tigris and Euphrates.

Words poisonous as red ants swarmed the minds of village men with intent to paralyze with greed. The taller of the two strangers, generous with an assassin's darkness, suffused treachery through every fold of the red cloak hung loosely about his shoulders; shiny rings gleaming bright, burning like flares from fireworks. Intensity of voice carrying wickedness, a passing wind heavily weighted seemed to sweep away light from the Elder's courtyard.

"We circle this village to follow our work of that night a decade

157

since; failed in our claim to treasure hidden by those we took away. Leaving the boy to the fire may have not have served our purpose. If rumors of his survival are indeed true we have danger of exposure."

The other's laughter flickered with sinister notes that caught to the shutter's encasement. *"None survived our power that night. All was consumed as testament to our strength; fire minion to our command taking their miserable little house."* It may have been arrogance which blinded their strange sight within the crumbling walls of the lost house where the charred bones of a tall blue cupboard yet survived; leaning as if in grief.

"If the boy lived, we would see fear creeping under deceptions of these villagers thus opening the price we would exact for thwarting our purpose to claim the certainty the boy's parents died for."

The brother curled tight against the evil that had sent flames cutting through the dark of sky that night a decade past. Cringing at the poisonous words that played outside the tired shutters he felt desperation in the need to return to the safety of the Elder who waited for him with his brother and Layth. The boy followed the voices vanishing into the suffocating dust hanging in the wake of his descent from the hilltop. The crush of low voices spewed venom, spinning out nightmarish visions before their grip loosened from the afternoon silence, escaping to the road's end, disappearing finally from the afternoon heat as if by magic.

... The other's laughter flickered with sinister notes ...

Stretching into the silence that followed he strained his neck to peer through the broken shutter, veering away sharply, buckling with a great thud against the wall when the men stopped, turning to look back with piercing suspicion at the little house that hid him. Stale breaths hung in the air of the courtyard holding him to the wall until time would quietly draw darkness away; Elder's words anew rising to his thoughts. *"Demon minds stained by greed, bent by suspicions, blight the very air we breathe; keep to caution."*

His heart pounded, strong enough to hold him firm in hiding from the deceptions he had heard; threat smooth as oil spreading across the sand, absorbed by the shimmering curtain of dust that rolled upwards in the heat. The boy had watched in amazement as its embrace swallowed the strangers into an unknown dimension.

He dashed about the house to pick up the rope and oil lamp. Freed from the risk of discovery the boy rummaged about making his way to a nearby open casement still feeling the shades of menace locked to his back; four hands, glistening rings, pressuring him to quickly climb out through the rear window. Trusting his luck to the protection of the curtain he risked to flee the village crawling from dune to brush to boulder uncertain about the power the strangers wielded, fearing to expose those who waited for him under the stand of palms. As the village grew smaller in the distance he began to run up the rocky path that had only this afternoon been a climb difficult, slipping underneath sandaled feet. The village was lost to view. He kept running until the path breached over the hill's crest only to drop him into empty space; body pounding in shock to find none awaiting him.

The knowledge of the Elder's strength waiting on this hilltop had protected him from the men of dark spirit in the village below whose voices set honeyed traps. All thought fled through eyes wide in fright. The boy began shaking into his sandals, panicked by possibilities of what might have happened in this place since his departure. As mortal fear took hold of him, he felt an invisible hand clutch at his throat, disabling screams, *"Be quiet."* Silence encircled, drifting patiently as he filled again with strength taught him by his Elder; thought returning to see the ghost of footprints faint under marks of brush stroke, eyes lifting to take in the life of palms miraculously come to breathe again. He felt the wind touch his ear. *"Listen to the whispers of palm branches bearing revelation. Close your eyes to see those you have lost."* The wind grew louder forcing his eyes tightly shut against its wailing sand and screaming. Broken sticks, grasses swept the grounds clean of deception exposing three faces motionless above a cloak of earth and sand.

The old man, first to wake from the sleep that had kept their secret, could see the terror holding the boy's eyes closed. Calling his name softly, rising from the embrace of burial, he reached out to break the spell reasoning, *"My young friend I cannot say for certain what is manifest here but I see your bravery has served us well. In our wait for your return, invisible veils that lie between worlds were lifted and those yet unseen guided us to deep sleep sheltering us from intrusion. Affairs of this day are directed by powers that seldom see daylight, crossing over to this dimension only in times of great portent. When Layth wakes to make his descent into the passage we may perhaps learn more. It is clear this portal will accept no other; our part being to keep him tethered to life of this earth. Let us trust in the grace of this place using the rope you have brought to harness him secure."*

With these words spoken by his grandfather guiding him back, Layth returned from sleep; the older brother following him. As they shook off the sand from their robes so did the stone quiver to clear its cover of debris rising in mystery as before without sound or effort, carried off in silence so deafening that none noticed its flight.

The four worked on to fashion the rope into a double loop to create a vest for Layth's slight body; back secure, arms free. The old man lit the oil lamp and passed it to his grandson in silence; his grip on the boy's arm conveying prayers of generations to keep him safe. Benediction solemnly received, laying himself flat, bent into the dark of the channel's mouth, Layth pushed off with feet and left elbow; lamp firm in right hand.

... a vest for Layth's slight body; back secure, arms free.

Once swallowed into the earth, his breath filled the confinement. Dark wet inhaling its heat pressed back on the boy, commanding he move only as a caterpillar might inexorably creep towards its death.

Layth pushed the lamp before him as the path narrowed threatening convergence; transforming in space between the flickering of light into a glittering bejeweled channel inlaid with thousands upon thousands of infinitesimal shells curled tightly together like clustered buds of vine flowers. Shiny they were, as stars in night skies, sparkling and dancing under the flame of the oil lamp.

Overwhelmed by what had come to meet him through the dark he laid his forehead to the ground, eyes closed in prayer against his struggle; opening to mystery. So close were the shells that he could see symbols carved into their spirals; ancient Persian texts.

Hidden within delicate glistening surfaces was the story told in every pulse that had led him here. Those long dead, silent for millennia, had left their meaning to the fathoming of story tellers who spun tales from truths; delicate enough to hold the sifting imagination of children, fine enough a weave to be unseen by those who felt themselves of large importance.

Lost in this way had been the wisdom of ancients but as Layth lay his mind and soul to reach within the carvings he understood these symbols as greater of purpose than a Bedouin boy searching for water could have imagined; changes in the natural earth would manifest leaving those that drew power from their disloyalty to her to pass from the illusion of their existence.

The symbols greeted Layth as brother. They disappeared into spiraled shells carved by the same hand which had inscribed the granite seal which welcomed the Bedouin boy to tunnel.

Slow undivided attentions egging him on his path down the channel until she offered her secrets, he continued to push himself forward by toe tip, thrusting his upper body onto his elbows. Presence protected him from threat that could weaken his journey; temporal embrace pulsing within these cocooning walls; each touch concise testimony that he was not alone. Energies here in collective, living within the underground complexity of divine matter, pressed on Layth, releasing him to move forward. He felt the instant of his birth within this space; losing sound and mind sight of those who waited above as he left behind need of his grandfather's courage to be embraced by the power that moved him.

Captive, unable to turn around, peace grew to consume his every fear of what might await just beyond reach of his hand through the wall of darkness. Compelled to draw forward over sharp rocks and crumbling earth, toes and elbows marked passage, lamp in hand; thoughts springing against the walls of his mind, racing ahead to where breathing would be labored. As he inched forward, he found the air meeting him to be clean, flowing easily in denial of expectation.

In the endless middle of his journey the channel shifted shape, his inner world gently changing its ever fluctuating planes, dropping to an uneven surface. The flame of the oil lamp flickering to a leap, flashed to touch the ceiling that had now risen well beyond reach; bursts of light bouncing off walls, reflecting in thousands of crystalline webs strung to glistening surfaces. Fragmented strings sparkling with intensity, filaments dancing in the air, rushed from the tunnel's shaft to strike his eyes closed; stinging lids so veiled in red that he would one day liken this to staring into the mid-day sun leaving him to see nothing.

The channel Layth had entered was portal to a realm where humanity touched the divine; *Alam al-Mithal* understood by scholarly minds as the hall into which human spirit could rise; the place within which those of the divine could share human understanding. Scholarship explored the terrain of this place that was no-where on the earth yet held keys to divine knowing. Within the recesses of this boy's soul was a heart in possession of its own key forged within warm deep oceans of sorrow, love hidden from the light of day.

Into this blindness sharp lights appeared sparking swirls in then out; splits of fire spinning to rise wildly in size forming two penetrating spheres which filled the centre of sight. Layth scrambled to his knees in the space that had opened before him, lifting one knee to standing.

Whoever had taken him through lifetimes since the voices had woken him that morning would shatter his every belief, breaking boundaries of limit through fear alone, leaving Layth the certainty of great power watching over him. Looming in the black recesses of cutting brilliance he could but discern other spirit shapes beginning to form in configurations of finite lines. Courage ascending to meet this new teaching, eyes clear, recognition widened in stunning heartbreak. Shock stifling him, silence opened into the radiant faces of those he most treasured, his mother and father.

LION OF PERSIA

.

Mirror Fragments
Chapter VIII

Chapter Eight
Mirror Fragments

The Castle on the Hill

Paused in the diffusion of pale morning light, the Chessman's eyes sparkled aquamarine with childlike delight from inside the crinkled edges of his feathered collar. Outside in the hall wet shoes creaked, he in his bedchambers listened intently as the Duchess Lady Laura Bennington caught Imled's attention, stopping her from turning to the crack of his bedroom door where he waited for assistance in securing his vestments. The crevice's aperture grew in size, gifting musical tones to spill on the toe shuffles the apparition had left behind; imprints scratched to the carpet's pile.

Responding to the music, Imled peeked through to discern shifting lights moving about slowly, her teacher's head cocked in observance, ear tilted in anticipation of what would announce from the speakers hovering the bed posts; the Chessman clearly immersed in what tipped his ear. Warmth reflected in spill of light, childhood memories flowing out; file after file of muffled noises filling to every corner of the chamber room.

As the door pulled closed behind her, Imled walked into the enigmatic sounds to see her teacher shift demeanor from morning preparations to the keen observation of the alchemist he was, intent on unseen focus; turning to the emptiness that had radiated to his back motioning, *"Come in;"* long gold diamond nails flickering; signaling frustration with flames stolen from a candle's light.

Shared with him daily by his small computer, perched precariously on the piles of books strewn across his night table, were long term memories and dreams harvested from a time he enjoyed in the simple indulgence of loved ones, friends, years liberating; perfections from a stroll through a flower garden. This morning a different light percolated through the Chessman. Preparing himself to walk the Spider Garden, he stopped a moment, shuddering as the chambers saturated with sadness; altered truth holding his breath since youth to a sorrow he had not thought to revisit in these last days in the castle. He looked about his quarters to steady himself; the room pulsing deep to its purple walls.

He was but ten years again, taken into the shadows of one early evening's descent on stairs leading down to dinner; nail heads lifting from linoleum to catch woolen socks knitted by Mother imperiling flight from the familiar haunts of old darkness. Intrusion filled the hall with the stench of new death that would tear into the living room from the television; warning heard from the broken voice of the man who covered the early evening news.

... with the stench of new death
that would tear into the living room
from the television ...

The Chessman, suspended in the fracture separating existence, was blinded by the explosion of lighting flare discharged from blackened skies of that night. Pinwheels tumbled in spheres of fire felling the tree that had stood sentry to the living room windows, allowing evil to ignite the glass bubble of the television shaking from bullets shattering promise.

The unexpected flash of a camera that late November now pulled him away from the robot arm that gently applied the rim of black kohl rendered superficial by the computer's history lesson; childhood trauma wringing out resistance to truth, his lifetime's work to contain what had been trapped in a young boy's person. Near to tears, fraught, heart brought to sleeve by emotions erupting; assailed by compassion he understood that all victories carried cost. The Garden of the Spider God still awaited his walk; its labyrinthine corridors keeping hidden the parallel worlds wherein alternate dimensions worked in peace and safety to birth Earth's destiny protected from insidious malevolence; the New Golden Age undeniable.

The terminal continued accessing information through silver threads linking him to disturbing visions of boyhood. He picked up the last of the crystal encrusted finger claws, slipping it to the tip of the right thumb of his bone white hands just as the President's motorcade came to a standstill on the projected screen.

...pulled him away from the robot arm
that gently applied the rim of black kohl

His breathing blinked at the image then started, filling deeply to press behind his eyes. Taken aback, his shoulders rose to drop again as sorrows the Chessman thought long gone waited again in defeat.

These images were drawn from his store of memories; shelved by digital alchemy to be given new life on this day of reckoning. Succumbing to computer's direction, he accepted the need to return to the first of the many assassinations that would inform the arc of his life but elected his choice in how the teaching would be entered.

Closing his lids, he opened his senses to the indescribable warmth of Yorkshire puddings filling memory with the blessings of his grandmother's cooking; the dinner table holding still in anticipation of her famed roast crowning the vinyl cloth, cracklings of fat glistening like jewels, sizzling drops and splashes on the stove's belly dinnertime heralds welcomed on a night that promised of winter to come.

Memory entered that long ago room through tantalizing odors, continuing escort through the kitchen into the cries that deadened silence from those in the television room; six o'clock newsman rushing past to call his grandmother from the kitchen to stand at his back. Not knowing English, beloved Alice knew too much pain in her life to not understand tragedy; six minutes of film footage documenting the end of times.

Chairs and sofas bordering the room sat empty; cushions lifting empty corners under the weight of seated ghosts perched in disbelief. Old braided carpet, masterfully turned from old rags, looked through blueberry stains, dried as blood, at the little boy who shivered in a chilling cold of loss incomprehensible even as it grew to encompass others, messengers, agents so loved, respected, to have initiated the turning that would complete the embodiment of elements brought from the Magus, the jeweled circlet spun of earth, air, wind and fire.

Grieving violent deaths were those who believed legacies of action left more than simple marks on humankind, contributing to build a universal ark of such proportions that parallel worlds would crest oceans of consciousness; revealing human frailties, striking them with compassion and wisdom. Those jeering the humanity of messengers, giving awkward steps as reason enough to discount teachings of grace, clutching at sticks and stones as if to build empires, would fall to flood waters. Anger of ancients would wash over those who gripped in dying hands the learning of hatred and separation which privileged themselves as victim.

The Chessman, tired of the machine's direction, looked deep into the mirror, his reflection baring disquiet at what might follow this day of transmigration; faith in decades of his studies and practices notwithstanding that the maze of human choice would blunder the clear path possible. Alchemist, professor of physics, healer of bodies, the sentinel in service to changes larger than one life could see only what he could see.

Morning had entered with the flush of anticipation; music, incense and ritual to fill the Castle as Initiate transformed to Teacher, Chessman to Initiate of higher order. Memories drawn from storage stepped through a life of preparation; loneliness carrying destiny, love that created strength, insights that drew him on, scrolls of a life bringing the young boy into this chamber. In such accounting, questions raised in the violence of human experience opened requisite for solutions to be enacted, study left uncompleted.

The Chessman, tiring of the machine's direction towards contemplation through such childhood memories, chose for action, turning back to the dressing glass and calling, "Arm, Kohl please, I have a garden to tend to." He motioned Imled to *L'Enfant Terrible*, the wig that rested on the stand to the left of the perfumer's case. With her help they would start the day of ending.

*L'Enfant Terrible,
the wig that rested on the stand
to the left of the perfumer's case.*

Persia 1837; the Layth story continues ....

The man he felt he had matured to be, died that instant, swept away in a torrent of thoughts defined in secreted tears; emotions deeply rooted in the remembrance of a life shared for a time immeasurably small. Reunited with his parents, he was a boy again. The hours passed on a hilltop protected, palm shadows filled to overflowing with unparalleled magic left him numb, staggering from vision to vision, chained in a world Layth believed to be pinnacles of dreams. Seeing his parents, sun flares emanating to light this place carved deep out of stone beneath the sands was beyond anything imaginable.

His journey down the shell-laced channel had emptied him into this place most unbearable, borne again to the impossible warmth of a love unconditional. Agonies of memory threatened to shatter faith in his senses insistent; believing the unbelievable leaving him in a want to pull away. The crushing need caged in his chest all these years; starvation of his parents' affections compelled a small boy's heart to once again be freed to feel arms eager about him, drink in a love not felt since that last day. Pulled by enchantment, lamp tensed in one hand, he reached for support, seizing a remnant of marble pillar that leaned in, shouldering him.

Seeing his parents,
sun flares emanating to light this place
carved deep out of stone beneath the sands
was beyond anything imaginable.

MIRROR FRAGMENTS

The spheres blazoned orbs of light radiating to the walls; birth giving life to shadowed inscriptions carved so delicately in form that ivory colored cuttings shone as blindingly as diamonds. Fragments of broken mirrors strewn about the floors reflected shards of ancient life, each fractured piece holding a single portrait come to join its others; ghostly figures brought from all dimensions. In one small piece of dusty webbed glass, Layth recognized the colorless alabaster skin of the tall male figure from his dream morning; hair red as flame seeding the sun from out of this darkness filtering light into everything that surrounded him.

Endurance had enabled Layth to navigate towards the truth of this channel, determination kept his mind centered to the physical, sharp edges of rock cutting his caterpillar toes as they dug in the fossilized bed to evade the narrowing passage; dark heat pressing on the lamp, tall flickers struggling to stay alive. All this lifted from him as visions released the burden of reality; mirrored portrait of the flame haired man revealing his long white fingers tangled in the mane of a blue-eyed lion.

Without earth-bound thought to blind him, Layth squinted through the undulating mist bound within the cutting edges of dark glass to see his own reflection settling behind the lion's shoulder, the essence of his being standing rapt in the fragments of mirrored dimensions; allegiance bestowed by a jeweled hand the color of pale linen resting in the mane of the lion. Layth felt a mystic breeze ruffle his hair.

The orbs pulsed, dancing in mid-air; points of iridescence flashing to permeate the spheres enfolding the holy apparitions. Within their whirling encasements his parents extended hands in motion slow beyond perception, growing to beckon he accept the gentlest of touches; arms of substance tearing him asunder. He stood awkwardly, gripping the cracked surface of his support; emotional pain shooting through him. With gentle cries in the faintest of voices visions reached through to touch his soul, lifting his very essence higher into unconditional spirit. Corners of his mouth trembling at the caress of his parents' love; smile paralyzed in an impossible tenderness.

Beyond the reach of speech, collective tears streaming from wide eyes; reunited with loved ones, they looked to one another through opened skies, liquid gazes blind to the walls around them. Strength of family lost to time whispered; unblemished crystals spilling to his ears. Ethereal cradle spun of gossamer threads enveloped the boy, bestowing upon him the mantle of Spirit now embodied; Luminescence speaking in affections, echoes filling every cell of the chamber.

"Captive we have been to this world of gods, watching these many years as ideologies of unconscious have guided you through hands of those

embodying ordained aspirations. If you believe as we do, this gift will hold magical powers." These words resonated, unlocking the power hidden within the pouch carried always by Layth's side. Secrets nearest to dreams, meanings awakened within desert mirages, words echoing the passing stranger set amber to quivering within the small goatskin. Startled by the vibrations, he reached to grasp the tightly wrapped bundle inside; fingers curling around the linen shroud to pull it safely into his hand.

"Layth, look to us in the way you have looked upon the stars, with the amber disk to guide your sight. The resin eyes what this chamber has kept safe these millennia." The boy paused to understand Mother's words before carefully unwrapping the cherished sliver of amber stone. Pressing it to his brow, looking through the golden disk as he was bidden, Layth watched the contents of the vaulted chamber heave with life; filled with a vibrancy undetected by the naked eye.

"We have led you here to the back of the blue cupboard, where once you entered through the open shelf in front; a plank left to swing shut against the harm outside. We left you that night and here we join again as you begin your journey; ushered onto the path we now walk with those self-same teachers who carved wisdom onto the spiral shells of the passage which brought you to us."

"Chosen by the Silence in parallel worlds to nurture the Divine Truth which has lived in abeyance since time began, our bodies borrowed, souls belonging to us, we travelers come into existence from unsealed universes to vanish into the Web enabling others of same thought to sustain belief that all peoples will

one day embrace the wisdom for which we ourselves have taken responsibility. In our turning as recipients of this universe, protected by the one Creator who blocks view of our existence from those non-believing, our task is to protect, hold safe the seed planted when the moon was young. Layth, you alone are of the lineage imparted this gift; tell no one of what you have seen or may hear in this sacred place, save your grandfather."

"Within these walls, an Age of Gold has stirred the very center of aspirations decreed in ancient prophecies. Encrypted in the stones forming The Hall of Dreams is foretelling of the day winds of force unlike any seen by human eyes will trumpet the landing of all you will bring into this world; giving it rightful birth. Child, you follow us in this line of succession as the critical link in the communications laying instructions for all others to follow. Through your work in this life, those from the Silence will reach out to touch this and other worlds; with our guidance intervening to bring divined truths from where they have lined these very walls since time began."

"Men, the living dead, circle the village this day, they who came into our home sparking fear with their dark fire in the way those of their number have destroyed light throughout time and intention; insatiable greed poisoning the governance of nations and the lives around simple hearths. Unbelievers; blinded by what they wish for themselves, unable to wish for those who might be brothers. They sought the jewels encrusting cylinders gilded by ancient craft not knowing the true power of such worth."

... looking through the golden disk as he was bidden,
Layth watched the contents of the vaulted chamber heave with life;

"Deception honeys the spread of false interpretations; consecrated teachings tainted with unspeakable distortions."

"Sins have led humanity astray, drowned in blood of those most innocent. The weight of such evil has held human kind to rocky earth but the future nears with a Golden Age that will lift humanity; your gift to provide safe journey for the manifestations of Divine Wisdom created with mankind's provident care for the opening of human hearts. Your life now is to carry the very core of the coming events into their power; guarding them with all creatures to help you. Look to your father. Set your eyes to those of the one he has folded in his arms for this little being carries the key to the moon and all she has witnessed."

His father stepped forward towards Layth who reeled from the sight of his beloved father with the unimaginable held in arms. The boy quickly stepped back into the shadow cast by the pillar supporting him; leaning away from the fearful touch of the unclean.

Eyes fixed to the fold of his father's arms, Layth did not see his father smile in soft portion, brow raised gently in question of Layth's withdrawal. He unfolded one arm to reveal the delicate splendor of the treasure held; a small dog glowing with crystalline light, nestled to the curves of tendril-like fingers.

Layth remained well away from the offering being reverenced him. Seeing the invitation in his father's open hand beckoning him come near, the boy looked up to the strong face he knew so well to find sadness in the quiet eyes. Resolve rose to meet his father's wish and Layth stepped forward into the light emanating from the creature.

Life suddenly woke, manifesting to breast; amber eyes beginning to blink, piercing Layth's soul. Tiniest of paws stretched out in benediction, offering touch unfelt by human experience in thousands of years.

Layth answered the call of alchemies, stepping out from the shadow to acknowledge the unconditional spirit of the animal; trust accorded only to angels. *"Layth, this tests the truth of your spirit for I see how your spirit overcomes suspicion and fear to untie what knots have been woven by misguidance buried in words; falseness of leaders."*

"When you leave this place, your father and I watching over you, you must go to the books of the Prophet, read his teachings carefully for the esteem in which he holds all life. Become the sentry he posted to guard the bitch about to whelp on the road to Mecca. Fear not the dog that walks amongst us for Mohammed himself loved all living. Those of minds filled stronger with thought to serve self than with faithful scholarship have usurped the true teachings. They must be shown the way of all teacher prophets; no one human owning this earth or her bounty."

His father stepped forward towards Layth
who reeled from the sight of his beloved father
with the unimaginable held in arms.

"The New Golden Age of which we speak approaches this world with shields impenetrable raised to protect those of like mind who gather strength to prepare her arrival. This tiny light beneath the dome on legs of four keys the moon; unlocking the secrets she holds to breast. Vaulted wombs around this earth have stayed motionless; pin-points of light under the rise and set of Moons within Suns beyond the mark of time."

"Here kept alive, safeguarded for millennia, the everlasting key to those who rise from the Silence is presented; unproved until this day reckoned the universal gift has lain in the dark breathing softly. For centuries undated, these guiding artifacts have waited beneath the sands brimming with awareness of unrelenting Truth; knowledge that humankind will pass beyond belief and unquestioning faith to fundamental acceptance of the value of all life without distortions of custom."

"Ancient sounds of lyres, heartbeats of drums and golden bells will fill the empty spaces wherein greed has roamed without limit reclaiming the prime state of existence from the grasping hungers which have grown to squeeze life from the soul of our Mother. We have guarded the portal for you, our beloved son, through which you will enter this sacred place to take possession of divine powers found herein."

"None but by your word might enter further for you now motion future reasoning. The faith in which all will join our living earth to see the Golden Age birthed in Silence rests with you to survive; cradled safely in your trust through this time of change."

These last words lifted away in supernal lightness; rippling away the spheres, transfigurations holding his parents fading quickly as do stars with the closing of night to reality or existence. Tears choked him with renewed longing. Silence wrapped around Layth, threads of ethereal melody woven through its molten cover playing to the walls which sparkled; relieving his spirit of the grief that had weighted him since his parents had been taken so long ago.

He turned to see beauty incomprehensible spread before him in the chamber as light from an unseen source shone as might the sun through vaulted windows; catching on the glitter of webs swinging from the soaring dome of the crypt to link every surface as loving hands might hold together in praise. The filaments that draped the dust laden objects moved in brilliant colors that guessed of vivid plumage; delicate wings stirring to flight. The covering of dust quivered to slip away as might a silken veil; counterpane keeping safe precious metals and shimmering stones tumbled to a myriad of shapes and sizes layered and stacked.

Layth's eyes adjusted to the blinding light which spilled from the chamber walls revealing a city rising of artifacts preserved out of time for this moment. Radiance danced and fluttered about the air in random joy, resolving into a spiral pattern that drew his sight to a table upon which lay a small bundle. He could but discern a cloth wrap, the frayed edges of which softened the outlines of a long slender shape propped to lean precariously against two large gold containers. Moving closer, he bent to study the curves which seemed to clarify into lines of the little hound that had rested in his father's hands. Layth wondered at the importance that would have this creature hold such a place exonerated amongst the treasures laid about him.

As he was held in the mystery, realization filled his being with wordless dawning until finally he understood how the passage had imprinted knowledge into his waking dreams as it narrowed to press upon him with the spiraled black shells.

This was the most precious of sacred treasures guarded here closely for millennia by the intent of powerful alchemy. Spirits had lain within this silent chamber breathing life to sustain one another until those appointed by ancient reason would return. Each would add its measure to open the way for the Golden Age but the small mummy given possession of a jeweled circlet about its neck would be laid in a sarcophagus for a larger journey to reunite within human experience; fulfilling transmutation promised, igniting the eternal flame which would light the rebirth of the New Golden Age.

... the curves which seemed to clarify into lines
of the little hound that had rested in his father's hands.

With such a confluence of power, there would be those in the world ravaged by drought whose intent would sense glittering wealth which they would hold in their grasping hands. This greed would blind their sight to the immeasurable alchemies entombed within these walls; affirmation of the whole of lives held delicately by Mother Earth destroyed in such harsh raking.

Layth held his breath, listening carefully as bits of crumbling stone and sands let fall from the vault's supporting walls. A passing whisper called him to look at a cascade of gilt scrolls, tumbled in endless rolls from their place of rest. Shelves had held their weight until broken, beaten down, pummeled by desert years. Like limbs of dying palms, they had snapped in decay over centuries under the weight of delicately inscribed wisdom. The wealth of histories splayed throughout the room in all directions to the base of the supporting pillars where Layth felt his sandaled feet tip records carefully inscribed by hands trembling with passions of learning.

He felt the energy that had carried him since that morning exhale, leaving him to sink into himself as might a sail empty of river winds. The light seemed to follow his fading strength into the shadows but left radiance enough to beam from artifacts held to a sturdy shelf.

... a cascade of gilt scrolls,
tumbled in endless rolls
from their place of rest.

*... artifacts held
to a sturdy shelf.*

*Reaching for the
indescribable beauty,
his hand touched the edge of a box*

Reaching for the indescribable beauty, his hand touched the edge of a box to pull away at a sharp prick. Sudden heat sparked to snake up his arm in a brilliant ribbon of light that curled past his shoulder, wrapping around his throat, filling his mind with the language of the ancients. Intense life hidden tightly within the objects of the crypt began to unravel, the crypt reaching out to him with all the wisdom and knowledge it had held for thousands of years. With the gentle strength of his parents sustaining him, Layth stood to receive the gift; repeating the words of his parents to center his own voice. *"Seek to know what you can see; manifest the breadth and depth of your inner self."* He grew in strength; mystical atonements, sacred words, devotions whirling within. Centered in the wild spirals of ancient treasures, the little mummified creature sat silent, exhaling softly as if in deep sleep.

A sudden tug of his woven rope vest jolted Layth back into the lucid world he had left at the outside mouth of the passage. In the farseeing he now carried was the sense of how the three awaiting his return feared for his safety. A lifetime's connection to them called him to leave this vault; a stronger pull rooting him to this mystical place where his beloved parents dwelled.

Torn between obligation and need, he watched as an amber bottle waved, teetering to fall from its place on the altar, rolling to his feet. Reaching for this offering, he picked it up; tucking the talisman into his goatskin pouch, knowing the treasure would sustain him from this world of dreams into the world of desert.

Placing his lamp towards the tunnel's entrance where stale desert air rushed down to meet the flame near extinguished, Layth turned from the chamber, kneeled to re-enter the passage that had delivered him into this place of healing. Transfixed by endless wonders, he felt to weep as his heart unlocked to transcendence. Facing towards the world he now recognized as carved of lies and deceptions, he sank into dread, breathing in deeply of the air that filled the vault, fearing the strength and wisdom new found to him would be lost once exposed to harsh droughts of the world he left to the outside.

Drowned by emotions, he flushed with thoughts mixed of bitter and sweet; powerful love striking to release pain stored away. Layth's initiation to secrets deep as the chamber room itself filled him with a strange peace separating him from those tending the rope tying him to village life yet wrapping him tighter into the web of all life woven by the Mother.

The tensions sent through the tug of rope made him uneasy. Long deep breaths confirmed his resolve to keep this sacred place safe as by the charge of the ancients that now claimed his life whispering they would watch over those of the crypt until the New Golden Age would be rightfully birthed. Layth was now one of the treasures of this place with its knowledge living within him. Inching his way back up to the desert hilltop, he relaxed into the tunnel as the walls pressed to his advantage; offering endless scripts gathered for him by those Keepers of Divine Knowledge as they traveled unseen and parallel worlds; sharp stones moving aside to ease the work of caterpillar toes that pushed the boy up the channel, lamp in hand before him until the last burn of daylight swallowed its flame.

Holders of the Sacred Trust
Chapter IX

Chapter Nine
Holders of the Sacred Trust

The Castle on the Hill

Imled watched as her teacher picked up the last of the crystal encrusted finger claws, slipping it into place on a bone white hand she knew so well. Student, caretaker she had been to this great man; for decades watching him measure elements precisely in his alchemy, showing the perfect bud to prune for a glorious season to come, rolling pastry to wrap summer fruits, the firm hold it took when one of his cherished pressed by him to chase the garden squirrels. A tightness she saw in this last tiny fitting; subtle clue to a mind ruffled with impatience on a day attended for lifetimes.

This day had opened for her in the small cottage that settled life here with treasures of a young woman's far home set in worn silver frames and tapestries woven of sunshine lining thick walls of English castle stone. In the strong hold of this place, destiny entering through dream, creative ruler of forms and ideas, gods and demons, manifest as the earth began her final stages of rebirth; old regimes to be abandoned by a New Age, left to crumble, tumble, new nations to grow, rising out from their dust. Stone walls canted up to the steps of pyramids. Heavy brass gongs stuck; processional signaling arrivals into the Hall of Gods, divine beings of light, and the Mother, gathering in Silence as Imled watched through sleepy eyes; her slight frame hidden in the shadows.

Peacocks of brilliant white sailed through arches framing the moon; gliding to stop gently as a single feather on the checkerboard tiles of white and black that edged the Initiate's shadowed perch. Bowing low to swoop great wings in graceful flourish, they bade her enter the ceremony; accept the role for which she had been chosen.

Invocation summoned those who would guide Imled through investiture and tenure; induction formal in custom and rite across dimensions and time anointing her Caretaker of Earth in the delicate waters pooled in the moon. The young woman from Mexico felt the true statement of her strength under the watch of the Chessman; recessional voices of ceremonial choirs fading to release Imled from dream to sink into the comfort of her bed, endless light of ultimate beauty entwined from all parallel worlds drawing her into new life. She rose clothed in the warmth of numinous visions, dressing for spring early to the Garden.

She had crossed the castle path to be met by antediluvian blessing, released the castle hounds to the garden in joyous tumble, accepted acknowledgement of those in the portrait hall through her passage into this chamber where now stood her teacher wishing help with vestment for his own ritual.

*... divine beings of light, and the Mother, gathering in Silence
as Imled watched through sleepy eyes ...*

Peacocks of brilliant white sailed through arches framing the moon;

The hall clock chimed; monument to those in the castle, echoing the fading dream. Imled felt the passing of her friend cold against the memory of her own ceremony of crossing; emptiness in the place held by trust. Her friend turned to smile at her, impatience released.

"Remember I hear your thoughts and remind you also that we are never to be truly separate. We simply shall hold one another with invisible hands. The computer has asked that I consider fruits of great loss and perhaps I have given regret some power undue. Your face etched in wisdom and grace gives me reason to remember how powerful our cause. Many have traveled our path carrying the seeds of truth unseen. Unjust deaths have stolen time but seeds sown on ready winds will explode in colors of wild meadows; prosperity, a new time to humankind and the earth that nurtures us, a Golden Age I shall journey in the winding gardens of the spider god."

"Computer. Off."

"Standing here I have seen testament of depths to which a race can return without limit or thought to lessons clearly written in history over and over on the blackboard of time. Lack of self-awareness, wreaking damage to fulfillment of a single human life, lies no less destructive upon societies dwelling in belief of virtue and moral principle unable to see depravity in their actions. Like the small creatures running baseboards, we somehow have managed to stay alive, clawing at one another to separate worth by values artificial. Leaves of the kaleidoscope will curl and those insects hiding in the walls we build will yet in

future feed us."

The Chessman turned away from Imled, turning back with long tendril fingers lifting a bejeweled Venetian mask to his face; the bird he favored during *Carnevale* in the floating city he so loved.

"Such a dear servant this little bird of mine; going before me to announce my anonymity. Freed of confinement by those who would follow my steps, I walk a free man; traveling lightly with no trappings of office. My journeys in future will be as those we have walked in the Spider Garden; communion with nature without translation."

"My companions await my crossing in the way of theirs. As I watched them greet your passage this morning, I could see my place readied in the hall; the castle having graciously made room ample for the sweep of my robes. The gold of the frame I see is wet and so it seems we are to leave time for gilt to set. Come, we will dance in the Garden for Spring trills her arrival. The earth stretches in the last hours of dark. Reminded I have been of her children lost; messengers of her beauty and grace, spirit and nature transcendent and inseparable."

"Sorrow left in the passing of the great can turn furrows readied for new planting. Such sorrow pulls down at spirit merely as prelude to flight for those whose hearts are set to the stars; the archer pulling back the arrow to send it into the heavens. Where people's sight is short, there is no aim to carry the lives of those teachers into the New Age. Honor is most profound in actions that echo the steps of the Visionary."

The Chessman tweaked the beak of his mask, pulling it away from his twinkling eyes; vestiges of uncertainty burned away by the light carried in the soul before him. Looking past the present, he saw the young woman whose bones knew tropical heats, her shawls layered against the damp of the castle. The burdens of destiny unrecognized had tormented her time as a child; insights beyond understanding tossing her balance loose, rendering her skittish as a trembling foal. Bravery found in innocence gave birth to her courage of intuition in the choice to leave her home to find her family here in the castle grounds.

The Bedouin's empathy knew her feelings of separation, having carried his pain in a small boy's understanding until released by the Stone of Ea. The Duchess carried like grace in her being; trust to frame an Initiate's learning. The American who dressed in city elegance had walked the jungle paths and dipped into the very *cenotes* that had sustained Imled as a lonely child.

The Magus had witnessed her arrival in the Castle from his chambers so long ago; parchments inscribed with prophesy of this day when the Chessman was to join him.

Imled turned the riotous wig in her hands, opening the cap to accept the Chessman's head in its firm grasp. With fitting in place, she tucked the few wiry strands under the band and gently turned her guide and mentor to the mirror centered on the

The Chessman,
tired of the machine's direction,
looked deep into the mirror, his reflection baring disquiet ...

dressing table reflecting the portraits where his visage was alive framed by French baroque gilt.

An instant split to see the blinding energy of a star light the room. So piercing were its beams radiating from the Chessman's face that Imled could but bear what streamed from the glowing jeweled skirts and bodice he wore; earthly majesty staggering, ultimate invocation possessed.

The highest of bodies presented itself; ether, the fifth element striking the supernatural to the old man's power. Wisdom steamed fire from within his breast to engulf Imled; pouring his world to be now of hers, gift of all Initiates streaming from the core of his being. Love profound for the earth and her children become the strength of the Caretaker; sentinel and healer. Time flashed, the hours struck chimes across millennia, the chorus of castle stone sang into the cosmos and the little dog on the Chessman's bed woke up.

Maximus sprang onto ready legs, bright eyes set as beacons above a nose pointed and quivering for new adventure and breakfast. The Chessman's laugh rang in the New Age.

... piercing were its beams radiating from the Chessman's face ...

Persia 1837; The Layth story continues .....

Warmth touched his fingers as Layth crossed the portal into the dusk of the hilltop. Voices muffled by his exhaustion, hands clutched, tugging the rope, pulling him through the tunnel's mouth where he dropped his head down to the earth as if in prayer.

Face locked to the day's light, eyes blinded to the searching of the three who anxiously awaited news, Layth paused to let the dust dry his eyes of tears that held the voices of his parents. *"Tell not one of what you see or hear in this sacred place, save your grandfather."* Layth gathered himself, rising to face the screaming of the younger brother.

"Water ... tell us you found water." The brother clawed, gripping Layth's arm, releasing as his voice faded into the emptiness he saw in Layth's expression.

The old man and the two brothers had converged on Layth to pull his limp body from the dark of the tunnel's mouth; hope searching for its reason, finding nothing to be read in the blank face; the older boy turning away in bitter anger. Despair dropped them to sink on their heels; holding their knees to rock back and forth in loss; loss charged by shock squeezing cries into the air.

... where he dropped his head down to the earth as if in prayer.

The messenger watching the frustration coil around them, brushed away sand, carefully smoothing down expression of lies.

The Elder sensed something in his grandson's manner that warned him into silence. Anger forced the brothers into confrontation; standing they leaned forward to challenge Layth. *"The rope pulled and loosened, twisting in our hands as we clung to every move. You were gone for such a long time something must have held you. If you had not found water then surely treasure is waiting for us."*

They looked unwavering into Layth's eyes for signs of some redemption but the lids dropped, Layth sinking to collapse on the sands that grew dark as the sun fled desolation on the hilltop.

The old man bent down to study his small grandson whose head lay heavily; gentle hand placed to the cheek where tears mapped jittered lines from the corners of eyes fluttering to rid lashes of sandy particles. The brothers stared disbelieving, despondent frustration twisting mouths; chewing on expressions of anger. Layth's breath heaved from the thin chest; no other sounds to carry meaning from the mystery of the tunnel save a whimper. *"There was nothing."* Moments passed as he collected himself for the telling.

"I am so sorry grandfather; the tunnel just seemed to go on into an endless void. The ropes restrictive, darkness confusing. Thieves only could have

found the channel's end, their skill taking whatever could have once been buried down there, if ever anything was."

    The old man turned his gaze one last time to the tunnel's gaping mouth as if to seek answers; turning back to the motionless faces, two empty of hope, another empty of expression. The Elder could not read the meaning of what had passed since Layth had tumbled into the courtyard that morning. Tired now, he remained thoughtful but confused of possibilities. *"Openings so narrow surely would have stopped looters from entering but let us return the stone to its place before we take our own to home. Remaining here will do us little good."* He was to bid the boys cover the hole in the earth once more with the stone but shock held his tongue in seeing the granite had carved a row in the sand, sealing again to the tunnel mouth. None remarked on this as it seemed the stone had rolled itself into place; reality of spells and magical signs clouding rational thought with mists of possibilities.

    The four made their way the edge of the hill's top without a word, descending the path before parting ways; once again making promise to speak nothing of the stone or what they had experienced that afternoon. The older brother in anger felt reluctance to make such a pact, kicking stones, his lips parting for words that never came. No thought surfacing, he remained mute as memories of the afternoon left him; carried away by sibilant wind moving swiftly to sweep away threats such as a boy's voice might carry.

The older brother in anger
felt reluctance
to make such a pact,
kicking stones,
his lips parting
for words that never came.

Powers of the hilltop would not fall vulnerable this day to the menace of strangers. The brothers took simple leave of Layth and his grandfather as if having met by mere chance; all elements of mystical imageries dissolving into the consciousness of unheard seventh notes.

The younger of brothers passed the elder's house carrying no reminiscence of the terrors that had pinned him behind the broken shutters or of the dire need that had sent him on his furtive run up the hill; rope and lamp braced to his chest. The older boy, impassive to numinous experiences, was delivered untouched to the village life awaiting him; infusions of freshly baked breads floating from the sense of tagine spices, stretched canopy sighing, abandoned by those who had finished with the exchanges of the day. The need ordained for these two was fulfilled and so released they were from the service of the Silence.

With his own secrets secure in the life of the spheres, Layth watched as their company, no longer having purpose, slipped away from the amity borrowed for the afternoon's work; disappearing through a wall of burning sunset, their blackened forms flickering in the last of the day's light.

Parting from the adventure shared by all, Layth gathered what he would need to continue on his solitary path; resolute with certainty of what awaited his return sealed beneath the sands.

Turning from the village, Layth saw the richness of the setting sun pour over his grandfather's feelings of the burden of age and the day unresolved.

He took the old man's hand to support his crossing of the courtyard leading up to their old home.

"The visions of this day are yet beyond explanation, your flight into this very spot to stand before me as oracle, dust rising high into the sky as gossamer wings of ancient gods, prophesy fulfilled, its nature unexplained. Come, I must return to the prayers I left in weight of this morning to search dreams and those that summoned you to the aegis of our lineage." Weakened by the run, parched by the dryness that hung in the air, grateful for the shoulder his grandson offered in support he wavered as he approached the door to his home; not noticing how it opened before him without the touch of his hand. Stepping over the threshold into the dark, he made way to his carpet for one last prayer but Layth reached out to him.

"Grandfather, come. Sit. I must share with you ... with you alone." With this Layth reached into his goatskin pouch for the treasure he had carried out. The little vial seemed to roll in his hand as if liquid swelled to burst over a precipice of heat. *"I have brought the meaning sought, entrusted to me from those who reached through barriers into the life of our world; doomed without their promises. The tunnel led me to a place beyond imagining; into the arms of my parents."* The old man looked questioningly at the boy; fatigue dropping away as a robe discarded.

The energy with which Layth pulled him again from prayers, sparked in his pupil.

"Grandfather, you must sit, for the tale I have been given spins the delicate weave of countless lifetimes. Webs strung to protect miraculous gifts awaiting us in the living crypt; ancient inscriptions have sealed a life waiting the kiss of this day's wakening. The earth once more breathes hope."

He held out his hand, vial sitting expectantly on his open palm waiting for the Elder's admiration. The old man took the treasure in awe and held it carefully as Layth began his tale; lengthy accounting of that which had faced him beneath the stone of Ea.

The Elder sat in silence before the revelation of ancient truth; shifting slightly to ease the discomfort of body, moving to stretch mind with the recounting of all that had escaped the searching rays of the sun. The boy spoke of the tunnel tight to his arms, legs stretched behind him, taking him past the intricately carved black shells of the shaft to spill him to light in a chamber blazoned with diamond spheres; another world of treasures revealed so vast as to eclipse even the visions which dazzled the journeys taken beneath the palms that day. The boy paused in great silence, measuring the space his grandfather could hold within, before revealing the greatest of treasure; the radiant light describing the spheres, the miracle of his son and daughter, Layth's parents, alive to cross into this worldly dimension.

Layth had a supernal calm about him,
his voice moving slowly to carry the weight
of each chosen word;

Layth had a supernal calm about him, his voice moving slowly to carry the weight of each chosen word; oceans of tranquility baring every pearl his parents had blessed him with, whispers prophetic. *"Grandfather, when Mother spoke to me fear lifted from my soul. She gave me a life I felt to have lost; her touch so real, the scent of spice brushing my cheek."*

The old man saw that fear had lifted from Layth whose eyes held wisdom unrecognized. *"They waited for me, watching over me, never leaving us. Grandfather, we are of a line that has been chosen to guard this wonder we were led to. I was kept safe here in the village that I might ensure full passage of these treasures that they might key the future."*

In the flicker of the lamplight the boy sat looking up at his grandfather, painting extraordinary pictures of the crypt's vaulted ceilings, endless riches tied in glittering strands of delicate webs; visions capturing the Elder's senses with every detail drawing him deep beneath the sands into a living world; concealed for thousands of years against the insatiable hunger that armed itself with thieves to do its bidding, Hope. It was Avarice that sang greed into darkness cloaked in robes of men; intent upon netting the gold swimming in flames of gathering fires; reality rendered unbelievable by the tellers of tales.

Layth told how he was endowed as keeper of the treasures; tasked as guardian of the New Golden Age to come. *"Mother and Father left me to feel my acquaintance of the artifacts I was to shepherd. Gathering around me they seemed to push into my notice as do our sheep, waiting to be led until the extraordinary held me in place and I felt myself rise beyond the ceiling, filling with memories that were not of my life; meaning and import of each of the treasures as if they were of our clan. This may seem impossible to be real but I know now what is true, my home has awaited me beneath the sands."*

Layth told of the journey back to the surface, how in leaving the chamber of treasure, the wisdom inscribed on the shell-lined walls continued to fill his mind with histories that would guide him and all those who would be touched. Before his telling reached the hilltop, Layth paused to look at his Grandfather. *"Is there a teaching of the Prophet leading the army towards Mecca that speaks of respect for all life; a mother dog that may have been shielded from harm?"*

The suddenness of this question narrowed the Elder's eyes in wonder of why the boy might step aside his magical recounting to query scripture. Trusting the boy's lead, he told Layth the story of the dog whose litter was set to be protected by a sentry placed as guardian. *"Why do you ask of this now? "*

Layth spoke of the little mummy; small hound he was told would key the moon, lighting the way for the New Golden Age his mother had spoken of. His voice drifted away on silent thoughts of how the tiniest of paws reached to fill a void deep within his soul.

"Understand what may be difficult to accept on faith, Grandfather, through the words of Mother and Father and the revelations of the treasures, secrets of the chamber hidden so long, witness I have been to all of this; we two alone will hold this knowledge as the Keepers of this crypt, without falsehood, living for Divine truth, shouldered by the ancients themselves. The threats grow large with the importance of these treasures to all life."

An image floated into Layth's memories; a city such as he had never seen. The buildings reached for great heights as did those in the dreams of Babylon but the path that lay through them was wide and smooth, molten as the Tigris.

"Grandfather, the treasures are to be fed into many worlds, bridging lands over time until my life is completed in death. A new home awaits these precious objects in a place that is not of the desert but floats on pillars above oceans of water. I have looked through a wall of crystal panes, seen flower bearing petals of eight; a rose of our royal tombs. Behind her enigmatic blossoms they shall remain, masked in dust, until the web brings one from a far land to take his part in their journey into the ethers. Frozen in time this ghostly beauty crowned of birds will hold in sacred trust these keys we are to unearth; globe of crystal calling others to their part in this great task; playing out this mystery to worlds seen and not."

"We enter a new life as will these survivors of the past within the chamber. What has been so carefully carved by my father, I too young to understand, has led us to prepare for works needed in caring for the New Age as you have cared for me. Fear not for our village, Grandfather, as the ancients will

send bounty from within fossilized tunnels; waters following in trade for your loss to the people as testament to your place as Elder."

Sacred artifacts as decreed by ancient reason would now find their way home with the help of those traversing worlds; beginning the journey of coming events dawning the Golden Age. The Sun would win its chase of the moon whose beams counted the hours until daybreak.

In the comfort of the small shuttered house the two, old man and holder of sacred trust, set aside transcendence for earthly needs of rest and human dreams which would guide through realities shadowing the window's ledge. The boy to his bed first, the old man pulling blankets to cover his grandson; the last flickers of lamp light glowing on his face. Layth curled in collapse of fatigue arching from the strain of a day born of endless travels. The grandfather allowed his breath to leave its vigil within the sigh of sleep to come; watching the warrior fade to the soft face of his grandson, lion of Persia, framed by pale linen.

With Layth safe in the light of the lamp, hand to the table top the Elder pushed himself off his knees grateful for the relief he too would soon know; his old bones creaking in the voices of the plank floor he crossed. The coolness of the air went unnoticed to the weight of adventures spilling to fill the corners of his mind as he stepped through the pin streams of moonlight, grateful for the prayer carpet which had waited his return to duty and promise since the boy had pulled him away so long ago; hours that stretched across centuries.

The night grew long, whispers perched to window casements eager to impart further wisdoms from the crypt that had taken Layth into allegiance with the ancients; their voices edging to slip the shutter slats; further mysteries summoned from beneath the sands unfolding what lay ahead of them hovering for the end of prayers.

Rising from the prayer rug, devotions fulfilled, provoking thoughts leapt from the recesses of his mind, impeding the Elder's journey to the sleep his carpet bed promised. Visions beguiling and bewildered were snapped away by rustling moans from across the room. He quickened to see Layth's eyes fluttering rapidly, lips muttering of ancient texts, voice settling into clear timbre of a woman's speech shocking the old man's hand into silence as he moved to wake the boy who stirred as though to undo the depth of slumber, standing to cross the room, walking to the moon's dance.

The Elder followed closely to hear the words spoken. *"Look to the cylinders bejeweled to safeguard treasures; teachings of Divine Order parsed to ripple from the hand of the Magus, wisdom awaiting revelation since Creation gave life to humankind."*

The sight of temple priests lining the round of the vessel
in procession
amazed him

Bound to the spell of these words, Layth carried through the dark to collect the lamp, rope; his grandfather following through the courtyard down the road to the place of loss, the burnt remains of a young home.

The moon peeked through a light spattering of clouds to see the old man and his grandson arrive to climb over debris buried beneath a decade of sand, loose and crumbling. Layth placed his oil lamp on a charred shelf where it lit the bottom of the blue cupboard in slivers of piercing light through which he reached to place his hand around the belly of a pot.

His grandfather watched him move smoothly as river flow, clearing away a thick filament of web, brushing away dust and ash to allow delicate engravings to appear from where they had been hidden; obscured. The sight of temple priests lining the round of the vessel in procession amazed him; that in simple picking, the child would have keyed on the very stories he claimed were gifted him from the tunnel.

Thoughts and questions held his silence, startled by slight rustling in the clay, spark of light within; sudden appearance of a bright crimson color, a moth flickering as if on fire, blazoned to the dark of night, waking the boy, face radiating the red of shivering wings. Looking puzzled at his grandfather, Layth blinked away the cover of trance to eye the winged creature stretching glistening wings to fill the dark; giant fans to flutter in spirals, vanishing through a crack; back of the shelf, portal to mystery, Elder's wisdom filling the emptiness left behind. *"Such visions are of grace. Brightly colored wings carry those who have passed beyond life back to guide the living."*

Plucking the lamp from the shelf, Layth dropped to his knees positioning the flame to the plank which had swung from a rusted nail these ten years. Conviction invited his grandfather to follow the path laid out in light.

Once past the swinging plank, they pressed their eyes to the dark tunnel carved by one's father, the other's son, from the earth supporting the back of the small home. As they searched for sight, the moth reappeared in the shadows, its wings aglow; flame of the lamp sparking into sizzling crackles, catching misshapen tips as the winged creature altered, transforming into the likeness of the pale man haunting Layth's dream; crimson hair reflected on thousands of tiny shells curled tightly together like clustered buds of vine flowers, sparkling and dancing under the flame of the oil lamp. This antediluvian apparition, hair aflame, color of the insect's wings, turned, vanishing into the tunnel's end. Drawn to follow, holders of sacred trust stumbled clawing against veils of silver webs that barred a door framed in bronze. Beyond this portal, light stolen from the lamp arched from the darkness into the room, untouched for centuries, where Layth's parents had appeared; contents a myriad of shapes and sizes layered and stacked, the man of Layth's dream ascending a staircase, alabaster-face set in a halo of crimson hair. Looking back over his shoulder with the light of the flame in his eyes radiant with life, he took flight.

... light of the flame in his eyes radiant with life,
he took flight.

The Smile of A Bedouin Boy
Epilogue

Epilogue
The Smile of a Bedouin Boy

Venice 1927

The silver green canal waters rippled with rumours of *Carnevale*; locals and foreigners alike speaking of the grand balls and masques, never ending processions of elaborate costumes, gossip spreading like fantastical opera. Jonathan stood beneath the arches outside his hotel simply breathing the rain filled air; dreary day unlike most presenting in Spring when young sunshine would flitter the waters overflowing canal banks.

Quiet spilled to flood San Marco Square; watched over by throngs of pigeons clustered, clinging to the parchment facades of medieval buildings. In surrounding shadows, one could see flickers of white wing tips as they sometimes lost their grip; feathered jewels shaken loose to crown other sills.

Morning crept slowly forward, pulling tourists into the square to be met by costumed minstrels playing Vivaldi; Venice swaying as haunting strings filled the silence with song that seemed penned of magical dreams. Travellers, in tall rubber boots, began wagging through the shallows, tables set down for them on the carpet of water in San Marco Square, servers in long white aprons,

*Jonathan stood beneath the arches outside his hotel
simply breathing the rain filled air ...*

black trousers, white shirts and tailed coats carefully approaching, paying particular attention to not splash any of their patrons. Laughter twittered from grey corners that promised nothing of warm sunshine.

No matter the weather, this orchid of human creation inspired those it had taken to breast over centuries.

Motionless, Jonathan stood awhile; salted air heavy with mist folding over his senses, draping his forehead like silk luscious in its fall, dropping from his lashes, caressing his cheeks to spill the corners of his mouth; tongue reaching without leave for her taste; Venice savoured.

Her breath on his eyes closing to encompass all this city was to him; where time stood still and return would be welcomed without change. The breathless sight and sensation of her, reclining on a maze of pillars rooted deep beneath her stone walkways. Canals strung with hand carved jewels; mirrored reflections dancing on faded pastel facades, translucence allowing light to live, giving breath to inspiration; lifeblood of poets and painters.

Jonathan thought himself to live here. "*Is this rain on my face or exquisite tears to salt my wounds?*" Lover of this consecrated siren, his spirit drawn to this otherworld, he came knowing the ultimate essence of beauty might drown, succumb to the ocean's embrace.

A chattering of tourists growing louder woke Jonathan to the encroachment of New World sensibilities onto his soul's century dreams. At the fading end of a long corridor on his right, brimming through the thickest part of condensation, a gap gave way to hundreds of people packed tightly like herring, struggling not to fall from the wooden platform raised above the flooded square.

They passed one another, twisting from side to side avoiding touch and the consequential locking of umbrella quills. The skies of the overcast day silvered the Venetian waters into a long dark mirror reflecting the chains of shuffling umbrellas, balancing the jostling walkers as they crossed the pine planks that began to fight the disturbance as it undulated almost causing those crossing to tumble, stirring the crowd into outbursts of cheering; infectious laughter echoing to the tower of St. Marco Square.

As quickly as it began, it ceased, quieted down, the walkway normalizing. The travellers having regained composure closed their umbrellas, setting the file of waving arms to their sides as if nothing had happened at all. People wove in and out like blades of tall grass in getting to and entering the buildings surrounding the bronze horses rearing the Square.

He had travelled Venice many times and so knew to leave her square to its daily business; placing distance between himself and the throng of tourists which would only grow more dense.

Stepping down from the walkway to the south east corner he quickly hustled through another jostling crowd to spill himself out onto a back street he almost remembered from many years earlier.

The narrow little walkway was spotted with dozens of small cafes; enticing him to luncheon but smells tangling kept pushing him down the lane.

The felt from his soft hat drank up the distinctive smells of bread, pasta and pizza as he made his way to thread a complicated network of passages that lapped to the edge of a bridge arching into a different dimension of the city; civilization fading. Without light, normal colours of the plaster walls took on a mysterious shade. The welcoming scents of steaming kitchens fell back; giving place to a mixture of wax and incense strong and unnamed; Jonathan shivering in a strange cold, feeling lost in this city he loved.

At the end of the dark lane, he saw a tall figure masked in robes of deep velvets and lace who turned to look at Jonathan before disappearing beyond a shuttered building.

At the end of the dark lane,
he saw a tall figure masked in robes of deep velvets and lace

Festooned by ribbons trailing and chains of gold, over the sweep of a bird's beak bejewelled, his wig of crimson had sat askew; arms wide as if in welcoming embrace; robes of *Carnivale* magic. Taken by the invitation, the young American followed, pressed between what seemed never ending walls of Venetian plaster twisting to turn into the entrance of a small shop and the smile of a Bedouin boy.

* * *

the story continues . . .

Book Two
Essitam: Custos of the One Rule

A destiny has brought to our world not only Layth's initiation to the Stone of Ea, portal to the Chamber of Gods, but an affirmation that caretakers, Chessmen of the Golden Age, will cross time and dimensions to weave the dawn of wisdom with treasures of the Magus; keying humanity to open heart.

Under the watch of Mother Moon, destinies are seeded and innocence of one small creature holds the key to its secrets. A young American shrouded in grief held to an ocean's graveyard steps to complete the circle of power through the watch of a family of reclusive shopkeepers bound to guard our future in a city firing imagination at the confluence of earth, sea and sky.

The Golden Web, having strung its intricate connections into the deepest longings of existence, brings to light the Magus; drawing reality yet closer.

"Essitam: Custos of the One Rule"
arriving Summer 2014

MAXIMUS and the GOLDEN WEB

Made in the USA
Lexington, KY
21 February 2014